ADVANCE PRAISE FOR
THE MATURITY FACTOR

"When I began reading *The Maturity Factor* I immediately thought, 'Of course, of course.' This explains so much of what I encountered in my thirty years as a manager and corporate executive and in the past ten years as an author, consultant, and executive coach/counselor. The vocabulary this book provides for leaders and managers in all kinds of organizations, profit or not-for-profit, is *absolutely invaluable*. And the models it presents provide clarity and guidance for getting to the heart of both professional and personal issues of growth and development. *I highly recommend this book.*"

> James A. Autry, author, *Real Power, Business Lessons From The Tao Te Ching*

"In identifying maturity as the key factor underlying the pathologies of business organizations, Larry Liberty has created *a simple and coherent framework for understanding and improvement.* Liberty clearly articulates remedial prescriptions for these pathologies."

> Sesh Velamoor, Deputy Director, Programs, The Foundation for the Future

"Larry Liberty *gets at the core of why people and organizations flounder or flourish* — 'the maturity factor.' In this insightful and engaging study of organizational behavior, Liberty provides an integrated approach to get at the essence of personal, professional and organizational growth and development. He offers *sage advice and actionable tools* for all of us who want to grow in our work and support others."

Mary Hessler Key, Ph.D., Founder, Mary Key & Associates; author, *The Entrepreneurial Cat*

"Larry Liberty has opened up a whole new discussion about how managers and workers interact that leads to valuable insights. His developmental levels of leader maturity will raise some eyebrows that probably need to be raised. And, he offers insight into how to improve the situation."

Richard B. Miles, President, Health Frontiers

"Dr. Liberty has ended the search for what ails many companies. Business leaders consistently mis-diagnose the root of many of their company's problems today and Larry Liberty has found the cure."

David Hood, Vice President and General Manager, Dell Computers

"*The Maturity Factor* offers organizations a *timely pathway toward future success.* Cogent and holistic in his approach, Larry Liberty shows the way for any organization to enhance its capacity for breakthrough results by exploring the emotional and intellectual maturity of its executives. *A breakthrough book!*"

> James R. Calvin, Consultant and Executive Coach, the FannieMae Leadership Initiative; Associate Professor of Management, The Johns Hopkins University

"I love learning new ways of reflecting on old, familiar situations. *The Maturity Factor* made me reflect in a new way on my own experiences as a manager. *Fascinating insights!*"

> BJ Gallagher Hateley, co-author of *A Peacock in the Land of Penguins*

"What a gift Larry Liberty has given to anyone committed to understanding and improving organizational performance! *The Maturity Factor* is unique, insightful and inspiring."

> Nanette M. Blandin, Vice President for Executive Education, The Brookings Institute

"It is my fervent hope that all organizations — and especially governments and political parties — will come to better understand this concept of organizational maturity that Larry Liberty has pioneered. The notion that wisdom can actually play a practical role in our business and organizational affairs is long needed."

> Jeffrey Mishlove, PhD, President, Intuition Network; Host, "Thinking Allowed" television series

"Larry Liberty provides valuable insights to how we can become completely mature individuals in our business dealings and our personal lives. *The Maturity Factor* is *an empowering tool*, assisting our growth and maturation as people and managers - bringing out the very best in ourselves and our work teams - so we can more effectively attain our mutual and collective goals."

> Woody Ritchey, President and CEO, Delphion, Inc.

DEDICATION

This book is dedicated to that small percentage of people who actually have chosen to be and to act like "adults." In my travels in the world and into myself I have discovered what an enormous challenge it is to act our real ages and to behave responsibly. The numbers of people who have insight into themselves and have a commitment and passion for growing and learning are expanding daily.

This book is for those people, some of whom lie in dormancy at the moment. I hope this work can provide a spark to energize your growth to the next level.

THE MATURITY FACTOR

SOLVING THE MYSTERY OF GREAT LEADERSHIP

LARRY LIBERTY, PH.D.

THE MATURITY FACTOR
Solving the Mystery of Great Leadership
Table of Contents

ACKNOWLEDGEMENTS

No book can exist without the support, friendship and love of many people. In this case I want to give special appreciation to:

Breanna, Mercedes, Zachary, Sherry, Bill and Mommer who have continued to show me the meaning of "family"; Rhonda for a lifetime of friendship and caring that has been filled with generosity and love; Tommie Jay; Dr. Ron Mann; Dr. Kevin Slatery; Ken Sheppard and the Sheppard family; Col. Ed and Phyllis Kropp; Carolyn and Ashley Crews; Nanette Blandin; Stewart Esposito; Gina and Brad; Breese, Jen and Morgaine; David Hood; Kevin Lombardo; Carla Noce; Peter Walther and Lisa Smith; Shawn Kelly; Clay Worley; Dr. David Berenson; John Renesch; Dr. Lee Row; Tiffany Rodriques; Todd Baldini and staff; Sheila Britton; Judy Cutler; Trish and Bill Cusak; Jeff Crosby; Paula Carter; Karen, Jeff, Ashley and Kyle; The Breakthrough Team; Tom Diehm; Stacy and Hugh; Marty Holtzman; Courtney Lewis; Lindy and her staff; Diana and Kyle; Michelle Hughes; Gregory Root; Jimmy and the Winstar staff; Debra and John McCain; Pomares and Company; Steve Passin; Phyllis Koessler; Carmichael Printing; Martha Week; Woody Ritchey; Steven Park; and all of my unnamed friends, students and clients for giving me the opportunity to test my models and concepts. My deepest thanks to each and all of you for your time and attention.

Fame is fleeting but friendship is eternal.

I am eternally grateful.

Larry Liberty

Carmichael, California

July 2002

A GLOBAL PERSPECTIVE
ON HUMAN MATURITY

This book has the power to change the world. Let me tell you why. Organizations, particularly business organizations, have unparalleled influence on our society today. The business sector, and the economic system which fuels it, is the de facto leader of the industrialized world. This dramatic shift in global power away from traditional institutions like government has important implications. Never in human history has there been such a universal need for organizational leadership that acts responsibly for the good of all people. The hierarchical, top-down rule that dominated the Cold War era and the benevolent dictator models of some of today's republics are equally unacceptable. A new, more mature leadership is needed – no, absolutely *necessary* – to assure that our children and grandchildren live in a time of greater civility, less apprehension about the survivability of the human race and greater compassion for all people on Earth.

Above all, this new leadership must recognize the historic human transformation now taking place in America and other nations of the world. Humanity is in the midst of a species-wide "growing up" process. After all, we are very recent additions to the millions of living species on this planet. We have so much more to learn and so many more ways to grow. We like to think that we are mature adults. But viewed against the larger backdrop of evolution, we are more like a population of teenagers, trying to make it across the gap that separates childhood from adulthood. Like most teenagers, we aren't quite sure how to navigate this transition but we have a sense that it is inevitable.

There are so many similarities in our behavior. Like adolescent boys and girls, we form cliques but we call them "political alliances." Sometimes we form gangs (also known as "armies") to defend ourselves. We make rules and demand unquestioned adherence to them, just like the Hell's Angels or neighborhood gangs in ghettos. We struggle with our sexuality. We experiment with drugs, alcohol and all the other numbing-out agents just like rambunctious teenagers on a Friday night.

If you have raised children, there was probably a time or two in their adolescence when you wondered if they were going to make it - if they were ever going to reach responsible adulthood, or at least some semblance of it. You could see them straddling the proverbial fence - poised to become productive young adults or turn into rebellious delinquents. The next stage of our society's evolution will tell whether we grow up responsibly or turn into "delinquents."

Our success depends on the emergence of mature organizational leadership, and that is what this book is about. Larry Liberty has documented the rampant immaturity that characterizes our organizational leadership. He shows the crippling price that we pay for this collective adolescence - not only in our business enterprises, but in our personal lives and relationships as well. But Liberty also sees opportunities for humanity to grow up and become a more responsible and mature species, and he shares his unique insights with us.

Teenagers exist in a world of very short time-frames. Their idea of the "future" might extend to prom night or maybe college, but seldom to the years and even decades that lie ahead. That is the domain of the mature adult, the thinking leader whom you will meet in the following pages. Liberty challenges each of us to become mature adults. Most importantly, he provides us with a guide to developing organizational leadership in a society still in search of its future.

- John E. Renesch, futurist, business philosopher; author, *Getting to the Better Future: A Matter of Conscious Choosing*

INTRODUCTION

This book can be "an interesting read" or the road map to greater management maturity for you and your organization. It depends on how you engage it. Assessing your own personal maturity is a big first step. As a very wise sage once told me, before you can really expect any change, you must know where you are and where you want to go.

I was 22 years old the first time I glimpsed my own immaturity. I was in Brazil as a representative of the Peace Corps, waiting to meet with the Secretary of Agriculture for the State of Rio. My boss and I and another colleague had arrived at his office at 8:30 a.m. We wanted to make sure we would be on time for the meeting, scheduled to start at 9 o'clock.

The three of us sat and waited for two hours.

Well, at my age, doing nothing for two hours was sheer torture. My young colleague and I grew increasingly restless and periodically exchanged looks of exasperation. Our boss, more experienced in the ways of Brazil, simply sat there and smiled at our impatience. The Secretary's administrative assistant offered not a clue as to where her boss was or when he might arrive.

Another half-hour passed before the Secretary arrived and welcomed us into his office. I expected him to offer an apology, a justification – *something* to explain why we had been made to wait so long. None was forthcoming. He just smiled politely and began to discuss the topics on our agenda.

For the first fifteen minutes, I found myself virtually unable to listen to him because I was soooooo upset at his rude behavior. When the meeting ended and the three of us left the building, my young colleague and I couldn't wait to vent. I was especially eloquent in my condemnation of the Secretary and the entire Brazilian bureaucracy. "What an incredibly insulting experience!" I raged.

At that, the boss stopped me. "Wait," he said, "I want to know what you learned from this morning." The question dumbfounded me. But as I thought about it, I began to get an idea of what he was trying to tell me. All my ranting was accomplishing nothing. I was behaving more like an adolescent than a grown-up. "Quit reacting with your emotions and think what you have learned about the Brazilian world of organizations and government," he was saying. "Start with the observation that they may be operating according to a totally different paradigm than we Americans are used to. Consider how to work within that reality."

It was a turning point in my life. In the midst of my angst and upset, my boss, whom I totally trusted and respected, had helped me to begin thinking like an adult. Learn from experiences like this, he was implicitly saying. Build on them, and be better prepared for the next challenge that you face.

I never forgot that moment.

In 1974, older and wiser, I set out as a consultant to help business organizations function better. I developed models for self-management, change, listening, corporate culture shifts, communication, team development and other aspects of management, and used them in workshops and one-on-one sessions with clients. As the years went by, I began to notice a correlation between the maturity levels of managers and the effectiveness of their companies. It became clear that managers who lacked maturity drastically reduced an organization's ability to function. So much time was wasted trying to make up for their inadequacies. In sharp contrast, an organization with more mature management was far more likely to be thriving.

One day, an associate heard me talking about this and asked why I didn't create a new model to help people understand this issue of management maturity. The research and field testing that followed became the basis for this book. But I like to think that the passion that drove me can be traced back to my awakening in Brazil. For what my boss taught me then is even more valid today. In a management climate of growing complexity and inevitable change, the biggest challenge for organizations is to discover how to adapt, learn and grow - and then make it happen.

Throughout this book, you will find examples of persons at many different levels of maturity. Each is intended to illustrate how all of us have the potential to grow and expand. This is an important truth: that we can change. There's a line in a Broadway show tune - from a Bob Fosse musical, as I recall - that goes, "It's not where you start, it's where you finish." That sentiment applies so perfectly to the otherwise capable executive who still has work to do when it comes to maturity. Don't be discouraged and, above all, don't give up. Seize the opportunity to learn how to fully develop as a mature person and as a manager. Regardless of where we are or hope to be as managers, regardless of how mature and wise we might be, there's always more growing to do - more ways to expand and gain wisdom as the years go by.

One of the characters you will meet in these pages is "Tony," a composite of many managers whose careers I have followed. Tony's story is told in four installments, beginning with his seemingly hopeless conduct as an immature oaf and ending with his transformation into a wise leader. As you read along, think of Tony as your guide and, perhaps, an inspiration as well.

My hope is that you will use this book to bring out the best in yourself and your organization. If you do so, you will enjoy an enormous advantage over others who continue to endure the inefficiencies of immature managers. And you will inspire others around you to expect more of themselves, just as my boss did that morning in Brazil.

1

WHO'S IN CHARGE HERE?

Finally back home after two weeks of non-stop travel and consulting, I realized I was just plain worn out. My senses seemed to have dulled. It was the kind of experience we often have when we've been in "data overload" for too long, or have let our lives slip out of balance. We have trouble processing information, especially details.

But even in its tired state, my mind refused to shut down. For months now, I had been mulling over the implications of an intriguing discovery. Each of my client companies was quite distinct from the other, and the issues that each presented often varied considerably. But despite the outward differences, each had something remarkable in common: too many people in key management positions whose behavior was problematic and even disruptive. I reflected on what I had seen in company after company:

➤ *Top managers were often less competent than the people they managed.*

➤ *Workers were often upset by the behavior and actions of those who supervised them.*

➤ Managers and executives either could not or would not listen to anyone below them who had important information to offer about key issues.

➤ Managers and executives looked the part and said all of the right things, and then, more often than not, acted in complete disregard of the values and visions that they claimed to hold.

➤ Smart and competent employees were overlooked for key promotions and advancements.

➤ Numbing levels of inauthentic, immoral and even corrupt behavior often prevailed.

➤ People who spoke about streamlining, efficiency, reinvention and reengineering were the most bureaucratic and represented the greatest barriers to progress.

➤ Managers displayed a strong preference to gloss over the complexity, severity and difficulty of problems and look for the quick fix.

The pattern was so universal! But how to explain it? I ran through a long list of possible answers. I considered the rapid and increasing rates of change within businesses. I looked at the altered sociology of organizations, with Baby Boomers beginning to accumulate power and influence. I weighed the implications of our shift from a national economy to a global one. I contemplated the impact of the new technology on managers and other leaders. But nothing seemed to add up. I began to have a nagging feeling that all the usual suspects would get me nowhere. In my weary condition, it was too much to contemplate. I finally put the whole matter aside and rested.

SEX, BEER AND TATTOOS

Before long, I was out on the road again — and about to experience a moment of pure inspiration. It came at a technology company where I was conducting a team-building workshop. As the workers seated around me began to complain about the company's management practices, I listened carefully. This was not whining or the usual bitching about bosses. They were frustrated and upset by the seeming irrationality and unfairness of their supervisors, whom they expected to be intelligent, ethical and operating with the best interests of the company in mind.

After an hour of dialogue, I posed a simple question, the reply to which has altered much of my thinking and become the basis of much of my work: "What do these people — the ones you're so upset with — have in common?"

The room was silent for a moment. Then, one of the more thoughtful members of the group said, "Well, to tell you the truth, Larry, they act like a bunch of self-centered, immature teenagers."

I was awestruck. I remember my mouth opened slightly to respond, but nothing came out! I had fleeting images of executives in baggy teenage clothing, slouched behind a building as they puffed on illicit cigarettes, talked about sex, guzzled beer and dared each other to get tattoos. Of course! I thought.

The group looked at me and waited for some wisdom. None was forthcoming; too much was going on in my excited mind. Suddenly I had the solution to the puzzle that had preoccupied me for so long.

Executive maturity — more accurately, the lack of it — was the thread that connected all these companies. Virtual teenagers were running some of America's largest and most complex corporations. They weren't bad people; they had simply gotten stuck, mentally and emotionally, somewhere in adolescence. Their bodies had matured but their personality defects marked them as immature. Because, few if, any corporations had ever made personal maturity a prerequisite to hiring, the virtual teenagers had risen to management levels they were ill-suited to occupy. Everywhere, their immature behavior drained energy from organizations and sent worker morale plummeting.

Unraveling a Paradox

In the months that followed, I formulated my discovery this way:

> *The success or failure of executives in corporate America is directly related to their overall level of personal maturity, development and sophistication. Executive maturity, in turn, is a determining factor in the success or failure of a business.*

But defining the problem naturally led me to another question. How had we gotten into this fix? Why, after working with more than 200 of the top corporations for more than twenty years, including direct contact with nearly 50,000 supervisors, managers and executives, was I now forced to conclude that mature leadership was fundamentally still missing?

After all, logic would suggest that the quality and effectiveness of management staffs should have made great leaps forward during those years. The expansion of humanistic thinking, the tools for improvement provided by modern psychology and the proliferation of New Age ideas certainly led me to expect that managers would have grown in common sense, maturity and wisdom. But it has not happened.

There is an odd paradox in all of this. We have a greater number of successful corporations and businesses than at any time in the history of humankind. We have more millionaires and otherwise financially successful people than ever before. But the maturation process of managers has not evolved at the same pace. Consider the following symptoms:

➤ *Employee loyalty is at an all-time low in American business.*

➤ *Employee violence is at an all-time high.*

➤ *Turnover in the management ranks is expanding at a rapid pace.*

➤ *More than 100,000 managers and executives have been laid off or given early retirement in the last five years.*

➤ *The number of employee lawsuits claiming sexual, racial or age discrimination continues to grow.*

➤ *The unwillingness of many talented managers to take a new assignment if it means relocating to another city is becoming a major corporate concern.*

Obviously, several different factors are influencing these trends. But the factor that is most common to all is the *continued lack of maturity, proficiency, and professionalism within the general ranks of supervisors, managers and executives.* Much of this is a result of traditional hiring practices. Most organizations have only one purpose in mind when hiring new staff—find the "best" person for the job. "Best" typically means the person whose skills and experience most closely match the job description. No attention is paid to the job candidate's personal maturity except in the most extreme cases. The whole process has become so one-dimensional that the phrase Subject Matter Expert (or SME, pronounced "smee") has achieved common usage at many companies. Now, SMEs can produce decent results in their areas of expertise, enough so that their level of maturity is of little or no concern. But then they become managers or supervisors of other people, and suddenly their maturity (or lack of it) looms as a threat to the well-being of the company.

THE DOMAIN OF THE WHOLE

Cultural influences are also at play. We in the Western industrialized countries tend to be impatient. We want answers to our problems right now — a typically adolescent trait! Compounding this is our implicit belief that reality is what we can physically experience. But Eastern cultures teach us that there are non-physical and non-rational realities that often seem in sharp contrast to the physical. Science is beginning to discover the relationship between measurable events and the expectations of those who do the measuring, for instance.

California consultant David Berenson coined the phrase "domains of reality" to describe how reality can be experienced in different ways. He created a continuum to illustrate his thinking. At one end of his scale is the "contextual domain" – the spiritual, abstract and intuitive. At the opposite end is the "physical domain" – what we can touch, see, feel or experience. The largely adolescent mindset of the West is most certainly grounded in the physical domain. But Berenson shows how the contextual domain is actually the source of all creativity. This is the way the world works: the spiritual, abstract and intuitive side of man generating the creative forces that drive the physical side.

Mature managers understand this - if not on an intellectual level, then at least intuitively. They learn to operate from the domain of context, from the whole. Less mature managers operate from the domain of appearances or how things seem to appear and rarely get beyond it.

For instance, less mature managers may pick up this book and look for tips on how to make themselves look good, to become more clever and shrewd in their disguises. Like actors, they want to be at the top of their game when performing their roles – masters of makeup and costuming and lighting, skilled in rhetoric and scripting so that their "character" will come across better to the audience.

More mature managers will pick up this book out of curiosity, a desire to learn and grow and enrich the experience of living. Out of such beginnings will come thoughts and concepts that may well result in something tangible – like a new manufacturing method that improves the company's productivity. But it will start from that point of curiosity and openness, in a spirit of discovery.

DILBERT'S WORLD: A HAVEN FOR THE IMMATURE EXECUTIVE

The first time I saw a Dilbert cartoon by Scott Adams, I thought, "This guy is onto something, something I know and experience directly."

Dilbert expresses publicly what so many workers have long sensed privately about modern corporate life: organizations are often led by self-indulgent, self-centered, clueless executives and other managers. In other words, they are havens for less-than-fully-mature individuals!

Here is how Adams gained our rapt attention with a simple cartoon strip:

> ➤ *He targeted the obvious and regular incompetence of many managers, something most employees easily relate to.*

> ➤ *He skewered managers who assigned employees to inconsequential or pointless tasks that had nothing to do with core business issues.*

> ➤ *He made light of our incompetence to deal with incompetence around us.*

➤ He expressed the frustration and upset that goes along with trying to accomplish the simplest task or job.

➤ He revealed how unaware some managers and leaders are about what's really going on in their organizations.

➤ He reminded us that we'd better laugh at ourselves and not take things too personally or too seriously.

➤ He gave us hope. After all, if Dilbert can see the irrationality and silliness around himself, then we are not alone in our critical assessments of the workplace.

2

Building a
Maturity Profile

I magine boarding a transcontinental airline flight and
being greeted at the cabin door by the captain – tall,
in his early fifties, a hint of gray at the temples, the
picture of competence in his crisp uniform. His welcoming
smile makes you feel safe and confident. This is a self-
assured and mature man, someone you can trust. Exactly
the kind of person you want at the controls of a Boeing
747 for ten hours, right?

Wrong.

What you cannot tell from his appearance is that he
has the mercurial emotions and psychological frailties of a
sixteen-year-old. Inwardly, he is anything but mature. This
is a man obsessed by the need to be in control. Anything
that casts doubt on his competency or threatens his self-
image sends him into a furious rage. His craving for
recognition and acknowledgment by others is so strong
that it drove his determination to achieve the rank of
captain. If his outward appearance matched his inner self,
he'd be wearing baggy jeans, two earrings and a baseball

cap turned backwards. Knowing all this, how do you feel about boarding the plane now?

Obviously, none of us wants to fly with someone who is piloting a plane to compensate for problems lingering from childhood. We want the controls to be in the hands of a person who is focused on our well-being, not so needy and self-absorbed that others are an afterthought. In short, we want a pilot who is an adult – not only physically, but emotionally and mentally as well.

Now, most managers in corporate America do not face the life-or-death situations that can suddenly confront airline pilots. But the parallels are not that hard to see. A company that fails to detect the presence of immature managers – the virtual teenagers I described in the opening chapter – is on a glide path that can end in an organizational tailspin and even a crash.

So the immediate need becomes how to identify the immature manager and diagnose the extent of his or her immaturity. My proven method – the linchpin of my consulting practice for years – is what I now call the Maturity Profile.

TRY THIS 'SHORT TEST'

The Maturity Profile is a highly effective method for determining the maturity levels of managers. Each person to be evaluated undergoes an extensive inquiry into all the important aspects of his or her life and work using an online instrument.

If you or your organization is interested in Maturity Profile it is available for a fee. For more information, please go to: www.libertyconsulting.com or call (916)484-6463.

SEPARATING ONE FROM THE OTHER

From the beginning, my goal was to develop a model for determining when and under what circumstances men and women in the business world behaved maturely and when they did not. Or, to put it plainly, when bosses behaved like sages and mentors and when they acted like spoiled brats. I immersed myself in studies of human development and organizational development and considered how to apply this knowledge to the world of business.

Out of that work came the Maturity Profile, developed with a colleague, psychologist Ron Mann. It is a method of assessing maturity, but with practical applications as well. It allows organizations to judge how well their managers function, how responsibly they conduct themselves and how dependable they might be in a crisis. Essentially, it predicts individual or organizational effectiveness based upon personal or group maturity.

Key to the assessment process is my method of classifying managers according to their maturity or lack of it. I use a scale that progresses through four levels of maturity — Low Functioning Adolescents, High Functioning Adolescents, Young Adults and, finally, Wise Adults. The scale is based on the behaviors that characterize each level. Thus, it's an excellent way to understand what separates the immature from the mature.

LOW FUNCTIONING ADOLESCENTS

They are the most problematic of the immature managers. Their skills and behavior patterns are only marginally functional. They hide behind carefully crafted personas, their true immature selves emerging only when they think it is safe to relax their guard or when they find themselves under stress. They tend to rebel against authority and are often shortsighted and defensive. They frequently display intolerance toward people who are different. Deep-seated fears cause them to often react badly to situations.

HIGH FUNCTIONING ADOLESCENTS

Though harboring Adolescent traits, they have managed to develop skills and abilities that allow them to function reasonably well on the job, and even excel. Their tendencies to be reactive, defensive and rebellious are often less visible because of their success at whatever role or task they undertake. But their work competence often provides them with a false sense of adulthood. They confuse their functionality with maturity, and that can lead to big problems. In my experience, most managers are High Functioning Adolescents. Bill Clinton is a good example – a man clearly skilled enough to become elected to the highest public office in the U.S. but behaviorally still very much an Adolescent.

YOUNG ADULTS

They are "rookies" at being adults and are only beginning to accumulate the wisdom and experience that is promised them if they continue to mature. They might be recent college graduates. But they already have made great progress.

They are eager to learn and have shed much of the false persona that shielded them in their Adolescence. Their lives are immeasurably better than either breed of Adolescents, and they are much more interesting to be around. Young Adults are a pleasure to work with and to have as friends.

WISE ADULTS

They are the best managers. They have accumulated significant wisdom and experience, yet continue to seek greater personal development. They focus on solutions and the big picture. Not every Wise Adult is rich or successful in material or monetary terms. But therein lies some of their uniqueness. They are acutely aware of their own personal needs and values, and they have clear visions of their futures. Their "community" includes the world, not simply their circle of friends. They seek balance in their lives, so they tend to be good parents and spouses, less inclined to workaholism. Wise Adults are not obsessed by what others might think of them. They are seldom "outsiders," since they want to contribute to society and serve others, but they are always distinctive. Wise Adults make superb mentors.

I'll have much more to say later about the four levels of maturity (see Chapters Three through Six). But remember, how a person is classified is not necessarily related to chronological age. A 55-year-old manager is still an Adolescent if his emotional and mental growth stopped at that level. We are talking state of mind here, not physical development.

HERE ARE SOME BASIC DIFFERENCES BETWEEN ADULTS AND ADOLESCENTS:

Adolescent	Characteristics	Adult
Unworthy, unlovable	View of Oneself	Part of the world
Fearful, angry	Emotional State	Balanced and even
Situational, depending upon current impulse	Integrity	Lives from values
Always at risk	Identity	No longer in question
Force = depletion	Use of Energy	Power = empowerment
Avoids responsibility, blames others	When Causing Problems	Takes responsibility for one's actions
The "known" or normal = safety	Reaction to Uncertainty/Change	Welcomes as a chance to learn and grow
Born with certain rights/entitlement	What You Get in Life	What you deserve and earn for yourself
Uses to get approval, admiration and love	Nature of Relationships	Self-respect creates respect for others
Present, short term	Time Perspective	Strategic, long term

MAKING THE DIFFERENCE

I once asked an accomplished executive how she distinguished between Adult and Adolescent managers. Her response went something like this: "I look at a person's track record, the results that can be seen. I then find out if they left any 'dead bodies' behind them when they departed. Did they produce the results at any and all costs to the other human beings involved? If people were left emotionally and mentally disturbed, upset and stressed, I know the person was an adolescent. But if the staff was left excited and wanting to work for that manager again, then I consider the person an Adult. It's actually pretty easy." Like the Pied Piper, an Adult manager who is supportive and fosters learning will attract a loyal following.

In my own observations of managers, I have found yet another major distinction between the Adults and Adolescents. Their perceptions of reality are strikingly different. Adults seek out what is genuine and reject that which is fraudulent or artificial. Adolescents, on the other hand, live in a self-defeating world of illusions. At times, I think the Adolescents have everything wired backwards. It's as if they are traveling in reverse gear on the freeway, wondering why other drivers are going in the opposite direction.

Cynicism vs. skepticism is another way to tell the Adolescent manager from the Adult. Cynicism, rooted in hurt from past defeats, is a common trait of Adolescents. Having run head-on into a wall and suffered the pain of failure (sometimes over and over again), the Adolescents retreat to cynicism as a survival strategy. Their mantra becomes, "No matter what you show me or what you demonstrate, I will not believe you." Being cynical seems far safer than risking the pain of failure again. But in the process, the Adolescents lose the ability to feel positive about anything.

Skepticism, however, is a healthy attribute that is shared by most Adults. The skeptical manager may have doubts about something but is willing to have his or her mind changed when presented with facts that are persuasive. Skepticism is not a knee-jerk reaction like the cynicism of Adolescents. In fact, one of the wisest things to be skeptical about might be the fantasies and excuses that Adolescents thrive on!

All of the differences I've identified so far between Adolescents and Adults are fairly clear cut. But don't assume that the process is always that easy. It is common to be more mature in some aspects of our lives and less mature in others. We may, for example, be very adult about money or business but remain stuck in adolescence when it comes to romantic relationships. Or, we may be quite mature in family situations but immature in our behavior with co-workers.

Charlie is a good example of this. A senior executive who had risen through the ranks of his company from union worker to foreman to executive, Charlie was made a senior vice president at age fifty. He had a great family life, a healthy attitude about his job, was well-liked by workers, and was an excellent mentor for younger employees. But one day he took on budgeting responsibilities for a special project, and some less-than-fully-mature behavior surfaced. His attitude about the budget was totally out of character—cavalier, even arrogant. Nothing about the budgeting process seemed to hold his attention.

When I heard his surprised staff gossiping about this new and disappointing side of Charlie, I took him aside and told him what I was observing. He confided that his wife always had managed the household finances and he had never before been responsible for a budget. In fact, he confessed, he wasn't really very good with money. When the company asked him to oversee the project budget, he knew he was expected to be able to do it. After all, he was a senior vice president.

Together, Charlie and I discovered a part of him that had never matured. This otherwise very adult person was acting like an Adolescent, trying to live up to an "image" and unable to admit that he didn't have a clue when it came to budgeting. The story has a happy ending: Charlie was able to recognize the trap into which he had fallen. He openly admitted that budgeting was not his strong suit and assigned the task to someone more qualified.

The episode reminded me that the maturation process is not linear: it is a spectrum, multi-dimensional. It does not necessarily progress at an equal rate across every area of our lives. A person's maturity has to be judged according to which level – from Adolescent to Wise Adult – best characterizes his or her behavior most of the time. To do otherwise is too simplistic.

HOME LIFE CAN'T BE IGNORED

Finally, it may be tempting to think that a manager's maturity level at work can be assessed without regard to his or her personal life, like the separation between church and state. But it doesn't work that way. A person who is functioning as an Adolescent in one segment of life will undoubtedly be doing the same in another, although the behavior may be better disguised. The maturation of the manager cannot be separated from the maturation of the whole person.

Most people put on a certain amount of "face" in a work environment, a bit of pretense or disguise. They are totally relaxed only at home or in surroundings where they feel very comfortable and safe. All this is quite normal. However, Adolescents take it to an extreme. They feel an almost desperate need to cloak themselves in what I call a "work persona," while Wise Adults do so in moderation. It almost always ends badly for the Adolescents. Their immaturity inevitably emerges, particularly when they are feeling pressured. In those moments, there is no hiding their suppressed anger, fear and frustration. When they are managers, the people they supervise pay an awful price.

Behavioral scientist Daniel Goleman, in his book *Working with Emotional Intelligence*, warns that "companies that ignore the emotional realities of their employees do so at their own risk."

Emotional and psychological maturity is essential to a healthy relationship between a manager and the work force. Work place relationships are more and more intimate these days, especially as we strive for greater meaning, inner fulfillment and greater authenticity in our lives. When people are "real" with each other, the "work persona" gives way to the real person.

Achieving maturity is synonymous with living a balanced life. By that, I mean the relationship between our personal lives and work must not become skewed. We should set our sights on becoming integrated human beings with lives of wonder, joy and authenticity.

I recall an executive at one of my client companies who became so focused on making money that she totally lost her balance, resulting in a very painful divorce. So many managers like her on the so-called fast track are caught in the same dynamic, going on "work binges" like alcoholics drinking themselves into a stupor.

Yes, the pressure to let work take over our lives is hard for any manager to resist. But less mature people succumb to it far more quickly than the more mature. This is largely because the less mature are more used to being out of balance. Unlike Adults, the Adolescents have not succeeded in integrating what they really want out of life with what they are doing day in and day out. Often, they find themselves sacrificing the present in order to pursue a future reward. I saw this in many of the Internet start-ups where young people abandoned all else in their lives to work "24-7" in the not-altogether-rational belief that they would all be millionaires by age thirty.

The bottom line: each aspect of a person's life is a reflection of the other. Immaturity in one's work life is a sure sign that there is immature behavior at home, too. And vice versa. Give me a manager to assess for maturity in the workplace, and I can tell you the kind of personal life that manager leads. It's that predictable!

3

THE LOW FUNCTIONING ADOLESCENT

Derrick was a handsome man of about twenty-five who got his new job through a friend employed by the same high tech company. He was hired as a low level manager and seemed to be doing fine until his probationary period ended and he became a full-fledged employee.

Then his behavior began to slip. He came in late two or three times a week. Other days he was simply absent and had no good explanations. Some female employees began to complain about sexual overtones in his language and a general insensitivity. He belittled people who were overweight. Some of the people he supervised began to refer to him as a bully.

It was almost as if he had hidden his true nature during the probationary period but could contain it no longer. Before long, he was summoned by the female executive to whom he reported. When she confronted him on his behavior, his response was to yell at her and declare that he was as good as anybody. She'd better not pick on him, he warned, or he'd tell people she was making sexual advances toward him.

The company made a last-ditch effort to get through to Derrick. The female executive, who had kept her cool throughout, met with him once again. I sat in as an observer. When she told Derrick that he was being suspended for three days and outlined what would be expected of him upon his return, he couldn't help himself. He started raising his voice, fidgeting in his seat and swearing under his breath. Finally, he jumped from his seat, pointed his finger at the executive, and snarled, "Do you know who you're screwing with? I won't stand for this, you bitch!"

Within the hour, Derrick was out of a job, ushered off the premises by a security guard. I later heard that he told his friends he had been fired for no reason at all. The truth was that Derrick had been unable or unwilling to confront his own outrageous behavior. If he had done so, he might have been able to start on the path toward maturity — both as a worker and as a human being. But that is a big order for Low Functioning Adolescents like Derrick, and he let the opportunity slide by.

Profiling the Low Functioning Adolescent

➤ *Thinks, feels and acts like a teenager, the result of arrested emotional and psychological development.*

➤ *Dominated by feelings of unworthiness and poor self-esteem.*

➤ *Engages in self-destructive behavior (drugs, alcohol, gambling, overeating, etc.), an unconscious attempt to mask the pain of rejection.*

➤ *Willing to do just about anything to gain approval or affection.*

➤ *Clueless about how the world works and why things seem to go badly for him or her.*

➤ *Unable to effectively cope with basic life problems.*

➤ *Angry, upset, frustrated, hostile, fearful, and aggressive.*

➤ *Living for the moment, short attention span.*

➤ *Impulsive, compulsive, self-centered.*

➤ *Attracted to people with similar attitudes.*

IT'S ALWAYS
ABOUT THEM

Low Functioning Adolescents, by definition, are the least developed of our four management types. They might have adult-sized bodies and even dress, talk and walk like adults. But they have the hearts and minds of immature teenagers. They see the world in black and white terms – this idea is right or wrong, that person is good or bad. They are unable to make subtle distinctions because life and "reality" are such simple matters to them. They are predictably egocentric; they put themselves at the center of their own universe. Their world is about *their* needs, *their* desires, *their* impulses. Nothing else much matters to them.

You can hear their immaturity in their words:

➤ *Why are people picking on me?*

➤ *Nothing ever works well for me!*

➤ *Why is my life always a mess?*

➤ *I didn't do that!*

➤ *Why are you always so nasty to me?*

➤ *I don't know, it just happened.*

➤ *I have no idea.*

➤ *You can't make me!*

➤ *I have no clue how that happened.*

➤ *I didn't do it but I think Rick might have.*

➤ *I put the check in the mail, really!*

➤ *Trust me, I've changed.*

The Low Functioning Adolescents (let's use the label "LFA" for brevity) tell lame or off-color jokes in all the wrong places and at the most inappropriate times. Scatology and cursing are often part of their repertoire, delivered almost unconsciously. They simply don't realize that what they are saying is inappropriate. Social context is something they have not mastered. These are people who want to be the center of attention. But in every aspect of their lives they miss obvious clues about what works and what doesn't. Not surprising, considering their very short attention spans.

LFA managers will try to manipulate ideas like "empowerment" or "teaming," usually with the unconscious intention of gaining more control or focusing all eyes upon themselves. But their efforts often backfire, causing upset and confusion among their colleagues. If they are reprimanded by higher-level executives, they feel hurt and victimized. Sometimes, they retreat in sullen anger.

LFAs often spend an inordinate amount of time rendering

opinions on little things — like the choice of donuts at a morning staff conference (all I see are glazed? why no maple bars?). They complain if a meeting runs into the lunch hour but nobody has provided for sandwiches.

They are careless about the need for discretion when talking about company business to outsiders. They recite their problems and concerns to anyone who will listen, without first considering if the listener is someone in whom they should confide. They're so intent on complaining that they fail to see how their whining reflects badly on them and their work group or the company itself.

Their actions are frequently impulsive or compulsive. They are always looking for immediate gratification. Short-term pleasure or quick relief of pain is what they are about, not genuine happiness or true satisfaction. Their focus is rarely global or beyond the moment. They are poorly equipped to deal with complexity and are prone to panic, fear or denial when they encounter a situation that is out of control.

LFAs will do almost anything to win approval. In the process, they leave themselves wide open to being manipulated by those who see how vulnerable they are.

They have trouble dealing with the most elementary problems. Naturally, they tend to hang out with other Adolescents, who can be counted on to agree with them that things are really screwed-up and getting worse. Their behavior amounts to workplace sabotage.

Looking Behind
the Behavior

What is driving these people? Why do they behave the way they do? The answers are not that complicated.

Self Doubt

They are tortured by feelings of insecurity and uncertainty about themselves. Their state of mind is so fragile that the smallest event or most fleeting thought can send their spirits plummeting, as if on an emotional roller coaster. Imagine waking each morning to nagging doubts about your self-worth, your value to others, whether you're lovable. This is the typical way LFAs begin the day. The worst of it is their inability to find a way out. They are virtually unable to achieve a moment of grace, when they might get a glimpse of the other side — what it's like to be well thought of, or even loved.

INNER FEARS

Fear is the underlying emotion of LFAs. They are afraid of being wrong, of being exposed, of being alone, of losing control, of being seen as failures. But the fear that truly rules their lives is the *fear of being rejected.* Imagine waking up with self-doubt flooding your mind. Then, add to that a surge of fear that your friends or co-workers will reject you because you are so unworthy. It is a paralyzing combination. LFAs often overcompensate for this by becoming aggressive and even hostile. Their anger is nearly always a cover for very deep fear.

ALWAYS THE SAME MESSAGE

All of us have had the experience of mentally talking to ourselves, wrestling with our most secret feelings or trying to find our way out of a dilemma. I call the process "internal conversations." LFAs have a particular kind of conversation running in their heads, torturous and unsettling, full of shame, embarrassment, anxiety and sadness. The more it repeats itself, the deeper it becomes imbedded in the hard-wiring of the brain. For the LFAs, this is almost like being a prisoner of war — locked in a place that is hostile, unsafe and sure to undermine a person's well-being. Little wonder that they begin each new encounter with a colleague or customer in a state of self-doubt and uncertainty. As we'll see later, Adults are able to interrupt and mediate their internal conversations far more effectively than the Adolescents.

THE ROOTS ARE DEEP

I remember interviewing a potential client for an executive coaching project once. One of the background questions I asked was, "What, if any, was the predominant internal conversation that filled your thoughts during your teenage years?"

He thought for a moment and then, with palpable sadness said, "I remember waking each morning wondering if I'd ever make any real friends and would I ever meet any girls who would think I was OK. I was in college before I met my first girlfriend or got a real friend."

His answer reminded me of how deep are the roots of LFA discontent. They usually go all the way back to actual adolescence and even childhood. In my experience, there are two basic patterns that explain this.

SKIPPED-OVER CHILDHOOD

Some people, for whatever reasons, never fully experience childhood. For example, serious responsibilities like caring for siblings may be thrust upon them at an early age. Under pressure to make decisions that outstrip their experience, they do their best to emulate their older counterparts — adolescents and even adults. They never taste the childhood joys and adventures that are essential for full development of the human spirit, body and mind.

One manager with whom I worked had just that kind of history. When he was eight years old, his father left home, and his mother began drinking heavily. The little boy became surrogate father to a younger brother and caretaker of his alcoholic mother, until authorities intervened and he and his brother were placed in a boarding school as wards of the court. But to this day, he tends to be over-responsible and an intense perfectionist, both as a senior manager at his company and in his home life. And so his co-workers and his family must endure unpleasant behavioral traits which have their origin forty years earlier.

Lots of LFAs have had childhood experiences like that, trying hard to adapt and *pretending* they knew how to behave. But the pretend part was not based on any real experience. It was like watching a movie about the painter Monet and then imagining oneself to be an artist. Kids who grew up this way tend to become adults unable to close the gap between who they are pretending to be and who they actually are. The emotional and psychological footing needed to really be an adult is simply not there. They can expect to have difficulties whenever they attempt to:

> ➤ *Solve problems.*

> ➤ *Process their life experiences.*

> ➤ *Create relationships.*

> ➤ *Learn from difficult situations.*

> ➤ *Create new approaches.*

> ➤ *Master an idea or discipline.*

> ➤ *Be responsible for their actions.*

> ➤ *Receive corrective feedback.*

> ➤ *Confront strong emotions.*

> ➤ *Deal with significant loss or rejection.*

Taking Refuge In Adolescence

Some people are afraid of growing up. For any number of reasons, they are intimidated by the thought of becoming independent and self-supporting. And so, even as chronological adults, they cling to the Adolescent concept of "comfort." But their idea of comfort is not a positive thing. It more closely resembles avoidance: do whatever you can to minimize pain and insecurity. Find a way to keep negative feelings about yourself at a manageable level. It is perhaps an understandable strategy for someone who is constantly afraid of being publicly embarrassed by their inadequacies. But it is quite different from the Adult notion of comfort, which equates with *positive* feelings like pleasure, joy, bliss and contentment.

LFAs put a very high priority on this need to feel "comfortable" in their adolescent disguises. It is as critical to them as physical survival might be to an Adult, and they will do just about anything to maintain the persona they have worked so hard to create.

Remember when you were a teenager and how important it was to look good? Winning peer approval was probably more important than anything else. This drive - to be seen as cool and together - becomes a matter of survival for LFAs, which explains why they can become so self-absorbed, mean, and even brutal if they perceive their image is being threatened. To them, their lives are really on the line!

It's no surprise, then, that LFA managers gravitate to colleagues who share the same concerns, have the same insecurities and play the same game. It's as if they form a silent pact that goes something like this: "If you don't blow my cover, I won't blow yours. And maybe, together, we can fool everybody into believing we are really grown up."

Tony's Story: Part One
Beer, Gossip and Getting Goofy

Tony, the customer service manager, has been around some. Fresh out of business school with an MBA, he went from one job to another before settling in at the multi-national electronics firm where he is now employed. He supervises 124 customer service representatives, puts in fifty-hour weeks because the company expects it, and is reasonably well-paid. But in the five years he has been there, Tony has received only one raise and has never been offered a promotion.

He blames his situation on company politics, telling his friends that he is being punished because he refuses to "kiss butt." In fact, he becomes nervous when upper-level managers are present, but tries to have enough contact with his immediate supervisor to assure that he will be considered for a bonus next time around.

When he and his co-workers get together for

beers after work, they gossip about others, share sexual fantasies about female co-workers or argue about sports. And they complain endlessly about the bosses.

At a company reception one year, Tony had too much to drink and made brash remarks to a woman he did not know. The next day he found out she was his boss's boss. He tried to cover up his embarrassment by spreading the rumor that she had been "coming on to him."

On weekends, Tony enjoys hanging out with his old high school buddies, watching football or another sport on TV. Sometimes they go to games together. When Tony has his two teenage sons with him on the occasional weekend, he takes them along. Otherwise they are with their mother, who divorced Tony ten years ago.

He drives a new bright red Mazda Miata roadster, shares an apartment with a pal from college, and lives pretty much hand-to-mouth financially. He is frequently behind in child support payments and complains that his wife is always hounding him about it. "All she does is bitch, bitch, bitch," he says to anyone who will listen.

He wishes everybody could be as easy to get along with as his old high school buddies, who like to "get goofy" and let off steam occasionally. Tony can act silly around them and nobody will give him a bad time for it. He hates being around people who might get on his case about something.

Recently, he heard that his company had retained a consultant to run some team-building workshops for managers. He hates it when he has to attend some stupid class with other managers. He's already tried to be excused from the workshops, but the brass says all managers must participate. This is making Tony very unhappy.

(To be continued)

4

THE HIGH
FUNCTIONING
ADOLESCENT

Thomas had collected an impressive list of job titles in his years abroad as a corporate executive. When he decided it was time to return to the U.S., he began casting about for a new employer. He found a small company that was on shaky ground financially and presented his resume to the owner, who had been in a desperate search for a new CEO. Thomas got the job.

Within a year, it was clear that he was not up to the task. After the angry resignation of a key manager, followed by several confrontational encounters and unsuccessful attempts at counseling, the owner reluctantly fired Thomas. However, the damage had been done. An audit showed that Thomas had run up significantly more debt than had been reported. (He had quietly taken out loans in the company's name to pay his salary and even his family's moving expenses back to the U.S.) The company was forced to close, owing nearly three times as much to creditors as it did when Thomas first arrived.

The owner tried to understand what had gone wrong. While he had not sought a reference from Thomas' prior employer, the ex-CEO's resume had been strong and a trusted third party had voiced total confidence in him. Curious, the owner called the prior employer, who said that nearly the same disheartening scenario had played out there. And contrary to Thomas' assertion that he had resigned from the company, the prior employer said Thomas had been fired for incompetence. The owner's entire relationship with Thomas had been founded on a lie.

Thomas' story is typical for the High Functioning Adolescent (HFA). Thomas lied to protect his image as a high-powered manager, the image that he had spent so many years cultivating to look really good "on paper." The right or wrong of what he was doing never concerned him.

The good news is that HFAs are a major growth step above the LFAs, or Low Functioning Adolescents, whom we met in the previous chapter. Like Thomas, the HFAs are more sophisticated, often better educated, and can even appear Adult-like in manner, appearance and professional bearing. The bad news is that, like the Adolescents, HFA managers are handicapped psychologically and emotionally. They live in delusion most of the time and with lies some of the time. Like LFAs, they are likely to have experienced traumatic childhoods, burdening them with self-doubt and feelings of unworthiness.

But the HFAs usually have learned how to accommodate these feelings, at least in some areas of their lives. Their typically normal-to-high intellects allow them to see how things work in the world. Their personalities are shaped by a combination of that intelligence and an unrelenting need for approval (like the LFAs). They speak with clarity and say what you want to hear, but they almost always have a hidden agenda – to find some form of acceptance.

INFLICTING ORGANIZATIONAL MISERY

The ability of HFA managers to take on the coloration of Adults makes them especially dangerous to organizations. They are much more able than the hapless LFAs to deceive those around them. I was reminded of that while on a consulting assignment at a large telecommunications company.

One of the top executives, Paul, had a larger-than-life reputation as a person who could get the job done when the chips were down. He was also a bit of a tyrant, according to industry gossip. But when I finally met him, the opposite seemed true. This well-dressed, perfectly groomed executive immediately put me at ease with his relaxed banter, easy smile and personal warmth. When he asked me to do some team-building with his management staff, I suggested that we couple it with some executive coaching for him. He agreed, and I began to think, this is no tyrant and certainly not an HFA. Perhaps people simply resented his success.

But when I posed some routine questions about his life history, he became noticeably uncomfortable. His father had been a military officer of some renown and later a successful insurance executive. Paul remembered him as stern and demanding, frequently telling his two sons that they were not likely to amount to anything. At best, it was a clumsy attempt to motivate the boys. Instead it upset and alienated them, and Paul designed the rest of his life in a way that he thought would finally win his father's admiration and love. He followed his father's footsteps into West Point and a subsequent stint in the military, earned the MBA from Harvard that his father never had, and transformed himself into a successful manager. He attacked every problem with intensity, asked tough but pointed questions, and was able to work his way through a myriad issues in rapid order.

Now, these are all traits very much to be admired when put into practice by an Adult. But in the hands of an HFA manager, they can create organizational misery. And that is what I began to see in Paul. The "body count" around him was unbelievable. He constantly attacked and berated members of his staff (as his father had done to him), often in front of others. Even when he acknowledged that someone had done something right, the words were punishing:

"Well, unlike everyone else, at least Nancy came up with some results. But it's a sorry day when a person with only modest skills in this area has the best results. Frankly, I'd be embarrassed if I were the rest of you..."

When I confronted Paul on his behavior, he was defensive at first. His staff (most of whom he had personally selected or promoted) was terrible, he told me. They had never had a real manager before, and he needed to press them into keeping their commitments. They didn't think strategically (like he did). They were too caught up in tactics.

Now Paul's HFA behavior was readily apparent. He was mainly concerned with being "right," making others "wrong," doing whatever it took to get the desired results, and winning the approval of the company's top management. He was callous to others when results were less than expected, lost his sense of humor when things weren't perfect, had little patience for anyone who was still learning, and made unreasonable demands on just about everyone.

If someone on his staff moved to a better job in another department or left the company, Paul instantly wrote off that person. One such victim was his highly competent secretary of eight years, totally loyal and supportive to her boss. When she retired, her colleagues threw a party. Paul, though, found himself obliged to attend a meeting and never made it to the party. Nor did he contact her afterwards to say "thanks" or "good-bye." In fact, she never heard from him again.

At one point, I thought a breakthrough might be possible. I took him aside and asked him to watch while I "acted out" his behavior. I was bombastic, abusive, condescending, critical and admonishing. Just like him! For the first time, he dropped all pretense and became contrite. I remember thinking that I was confronting a hurt fifteen-year-old boy. I had for a moment assumed the role of his critical and abusive father, and he had melted and become the Adolescent that he really was inside.

We made some significant progress in the months that followed. He toned down his language and made apologies for his abusiveness. At first, people were disbelieving. It seemed like just another ploy to get them to produce better results. But finally they acknowledged that he was changing and began to thank him for it.

About that same time, I was invited to his home for dinner and to meet his family. I was shocked by what I saw — wife and children totally subservient, clearly fearful of doing anything that might upset him (the same apprehensive mood, I imagine, that his father had created). I was dismayed at how often Paul had moved his family (ten times in twelve years) without their daring to protest. I was even more dismayed at the way he was openly critical of his wife or children as the evening wore on.

The most unsettling scene occurred when I remarked on his wife's patience with Paul's long hours at the office. He usually did not get home until 8 or 9 o'clock each night and regularly worked on weekends. She smiled and said, "Well, we do miss him and wish we could see him more often."

Whereupon Paul began to rage at her: "You know how hard I work and that I'm giving my body and soul to provide for our family and make a future for our children that we never had!" I was stunned by the outburst. She quickly apologized to me for "giving the wrong impression."

Paul's face was red and his body tense. It was a telling moment for me. This man had made his professional life far more important than his personal life, and I would soon learn he expected the same of those who worked for him — both classic HFA symptoms.

A few weeks later, the company announced an opening at the executive level just above Paul's. It was a promotion that he desperately wanted (and needed, to keep his self-esteem intact). To impress senior management with his devotion to the company, Paul called a staff meeting for Friday afternoon at 5 o'clock and let it be known that everyone should be prepared to work Saturday and maybe Sunday. His subordinates were heartbroken, since they all had made weekend plans. One staffer sent someone in her place, saying she couldn't undo an already scheduled family event. Paul began the meeting by launching an attack on her substitute, suggesting he convey to the absent employee that her behavior was unacceptable.

Paul had reverted to HFA form, and the situation went straight downhill from there. Staff morale skidded and some of his best people began to look for new jobs. He admitted to me that he had fallen back on his old ways but insisted it was the only strategy that would get him the promotion. He was being driven by old behaviors and old needs that he could not control. We parted amicably but have had little communication since.

Yes, Paul produced results. But the cost to those around him was unacceptable. Like all HFAs, his focus was on what was in it for him and how he could win the favor of senior management. That blinded him to the harm he inflicted upon those around him. He created an unsafe environment in which talented people with vision, passion and commitment became his enemy.

THIS TIME HE MISCALCULATED

HFAs will do anything – *literally anything* – to survive. To them, survival means being in control, always able to manipulate the agenda to their benefit and never losing access to their power base. HFAs live with inner fears and doubts, but they will fight anyone, anytime, if their control of a situation is threatened. And if they sense that they are about to be rejected by others, they will reject first.

I saw all of these behaviors in Henri, the Swiss-born president of a software company, when I was brought in to help his managers with team-building. This physically imposing

46-year-old, trained as an engineer, was bright, proud of his accomplishments, and personable, despite a certain gruffness. His company was a subsidiary of a European conglomerate, requiring Henri to travel overseas on a regular basis.

He kept me waiting more than an hour for our first meeting but offered no apology. I concluded he was testing me. Henri had wanted to use a consultant from his homeland, but his senior managers had lobbied for me. I spent five months at Henri's company, during which he regularly reminded me of how successful he had become. It was a "king of the mountain" speech. At one point, he even volunteered the details of his compensation, including a house, two cars, stock options, and so on. The package struck me as quite generous, but he confided that it had been a disappointment. I finally realized he was bragging, not complaining.

That he was an HFA was obvious. His dictatorial management approach, which apparently had served him well in Europe, was on display for all to see. He yelled at people in his office. During a team-building retreat, he constantly berated his staff. I took him aside and gingerly pointed out how everyone in the room seemed withdrawn and fearful of speaking up. Maybe, I told him, it was a symptom of a kind of dysfunctionality. He thought for a moment, then said he expected me to say that since I was an American. In fact, he said, he was pleased that he was getting his points across.

Each time I encouraged open and direct communication between Henri and his staff, he ignored me. Each time someone tried to speak honestly to him, he discounted what they were saying or made inappropriate references to their individual or collective incompetence. Finally, I spoke to him more directly. I said he would waste his investment in the session if other people could not speak their minds without fear of reprisal. He looked at me and smiled.

"You know what the best part of being the CEO is?" he asked smugly.

I sat silently, awaiting his HFA wisdom.

"When I screw up, I still get to fire somebody else," he said with a grin. "Nobody is going to fire me!"

I told him that I couldn't continue if he had no commitment to opening communications. He said that was fine and that he had not wanted to use me in the first place. In fact, I could leave now, and he would tell the group the sessions were over. No, I said, I never abandon a group without making a final appearance. He blushed beet red as we stood there, him towering over me. It was the classic moment for an HFA — a battle of wills. Then, grudgingly, he said, "Fine," and walked away. I told his management group why I was leaving, answered a few questions, then said good-bye. Everyone in the room seemed crestfallen; a few shook their heads in disgust.

Months later, I learned that things had gone from bad to worse. Morale had worsened and the business was losing momentum. Henri was eventually recalled with little fanfare and given a staff job in Europe. His HFA management style, especially unsuited for the cross-cultural environment in which he had found himself, had finally failed him.

Tony's Story: Part Two
Rescued from the Brink

Tony arrived late to the workshop. He had tried all sorts of tricks to duck it, but nothing had worked. He sat at the back of the room, next to another, much younger manager he remembered as an okay guy. As the instructor began outlining how the sessions would proceed, Tony let his attention and his gaze wander, trying to decide which female participant was the sexiest. Suddenly he was aware that the room was silent and people were looking at him. The instructor had an expectant look on his face, and Tony realized he had been asked a question.

"What was that? Did you ask me something?" he blurted out. All the instructor needed was his name, to check off on a list of enrollees. A few moments later, the instructor asked if everyone was willing to abide by the procedure he had outlined. Everyone nodded yes, including Tony, who wasn't quite sure what he was agreeing to, since he had hardly been listening.

After several class meetings, Tony was flirting with real trouble. His inattention and arrogant air were irritating the instructor and everyone else. And then an unexpected thing happened. Tony started to take notice of the younger man sitting next to him. Kim was on the same managerial level as Tony and had joined the firm straight out of Stanford Business School. He seemed very wise to Tony, wise beyond his years. Kim's thoughtful questions especially impressed Tony.

When the two of them talked during class breaks, Kim's delightful curiosity about team-building seemed contagious. Tony started thinking seriously about the issues that the instructor was raising. Slowly but surely, his arrogance and complacency began slipping away.

Thanks to Kim's influence, Tony finished the workshop filled with energy and the first stirrings of ambition. These feelings were still a little strange to him, but that was okay. He started organizing team-building workshops for his own staff, such was his new found enthusiasm. But he also made sure the brass noticed. A little bit of self-promotion couldn't hurt. He just might be seen as the "rising star" in management circles, he figured.

(*To be continued*)

5

THE YOUNG ADULT

The Young Adult (YA) is a person in transition, the essence of an emerging human being. I often call YAs "Wise Adults in training." They are beginning to shed any internal doubts about who they are. Their emotions are dominated less by fear and anger and more by compassion and curiosity. They are less self-absorbed; they direct more of their attention outward, to the world around them.

In their relationships, YAs are shifting from self-serving egocentricity to a desire to be with more mature people and learn from them. Having Adolescent "fun" becomes less important than being with companions one can really count on.

Their thoughts increasingly turn to questions like "What do I value?" and "What is really important to me?" Values like friendship, honor, integrity and keeping commitments start to replace the Adolescent trait of masking pain with instant gratification. Their focus becomes more long range, not just today or tomorrow. Maintaining family relations gains in importance.

At work, the shift is also to a values-driven personality.

Being "out of sync" with the organization's culture no longer seems so clever. YA managers bring a commitment to their employers and to their jobs that is infectious. They want to work. They want to master their jobs. They want to be successful without sacrificing their well-being or the well-being of those around them. They want to produce results without compromising their integrity and their values. They are exciting and energizing to be around.

Self esteem is no longer an obsession for YAs. There is more concern for colleagues and their needs. Long term solutions become paramount; root causes of problems are hunted down. Short term, band-aid approaches are employed only in emergencies. Under stress, the YA manager is less inclined to panic or find someone to blame or avoid responsibility. Rather, he or she reflects on what is happening and what can be learned from the immediate problem.

A word of caution: none of these personality changes happens overnight. The transition from Adolescent to Adult begins slowly and takes place quietly. Mostly, it's an inconspicuous shift in thinking and feeling. Anyone who expects to achieve it at a weekend workshop will be disappointed. It really does take time. All the different aspects of an individual's personality must travel their own paths to maturity, sometimes at different speeds. Some take longer than others. So it isn't one big and sudden "bang" and there we are, all grown up!

PROFILING THE YOUNG ADULT:

➤ *Eager to explore the new territory of Adults.*

➤ *Possesses a healthy perspective about his or her relationship with the rest of the world.*

➤ *Has a thirst for knowledge and strong desire to learn.*

➤ *Embraces personal and professional challenges.*

➤ *Able to generate results.*

➤ *Can self-correct when mistakes are discovered.*

➤ *Intent on personal improvement.*

➤ *Imbued with an enthusiasm for work and life.*

VALUES BECAME
HIS ANCHOR

Watching Young Adults emerge as managers is an enormously satisfying experience compared to witnessing the stumbling of Adolescents. This is because the YAs have a genuine interest in learning. They respond quickly to teaching and mentoring; there is less need to set rules and performance benchmarks for them.

Eric is a good example of this. I met him when he was twenty-two, an entry-level employee at a large financial institution where I was conducting leadership workshops. He seemed a typical college graduate, full of Adolescent traits. Eric was intelligent and obviously able, but smug and arrogant. He considered himself "CEO ready." At the same time, beneath that facade, I sensed that he was open to receiving feedback from others. He displayed an easy acceptance when I kidded him, and we soon bonded. After a few months he asked me to be his mentor, and I accepted.

We talked about his thinking and his approach to work and to life. I shared some of my experiences and insights and encouraged him to seek out accomplished colleagues who would be willing to do the same. Thus began his long quest for personal and professional growth. Today, Eric is twenty-nine years old, the recent recipient of a master's degree in finance and moving steadily upward as a manager. His bosses have identified him as a high potential executive; his salary is in excess of $100,000 per year with significant benefits and bonuses.

THE KEY TO HIS SUCCESS?
HE HAS A SET OF VALUES NOW.

When we first met, he was focused on women, parties, dating and sex. Eric is now married to a wonderful woman, and they recently had their first child. I never hear him talk about chasing women, weekend partying or any other of his past priorities. And while more than half of all marriages end in divorce, Eric and his wife show no signs of that ever happening.

At dinner with them, the conversation ranged over business, politics and the financial markets, and they sought my opinion about how to best manage their dual incomes. The intensity of their questioning actually took me aback. Imagine a couple of twenty-somethings actually asking for advice on their future. We should all be so lucky as to have a chance to interact with young people like these!

At work, Eric is invited into problem-solving situations that are usually the exclusive reserve of more experienced managers. He's considered wise beyond his years, accorded the same credibility as a person twenty years his senior. And for good reason: He asks tough questions. He shows sensible restraint when it comes to passing judgment on others and is quick to remind colleagues to look for the good in one another. He looks for solutions that will last and makes sure that both short- and long-term fixes are discussed when a problem arises. He is not intimidated by a person's position, education, income or other status.

Eric still has Adolescent lapses, but small ones. One Friday night after work he had too much to drink and was two hours late to dinner. He apologized to his wife and promised not to let it happen again. Like Eric, all YAs are vulnerable to moments of regression. But what's encouraging is that they usually learn and grow from such episodes, just as Eric has.

THE EVOLUTION OF A YOUNG ADULT MANAGER:

TIME

The future is vivid and alive. It represents possibilities that only months ago did not seem to exist or to matter. What once was essentially a day-to-day existence now is enriched by visions of the future. Best of all, each one of them is becoming a normal part of the Young Adult's reality.

RELATIONSHIPS

Relationships are now an essential part of life for the YA. They create lasting friendships based upon mutual values, goals and interests. Each one, carefully chosen, has the potential to become long-term and lasting. The Young Adult no longer has time for persons who seem less mature.

EMOTIONS

The key emotions are curiosity, compassion and an eagerness to observe and take note of. This is a significant shift away from the Adolescent fears that once created such inner torment. Young Adults relish the opportunity to experience life and learn more about themselves and others.

Values

Values are emerging cornerstones in the lives of Young Adults. YAs know what values are and they are consciously working to define and refine their own personal ethics and values. They see values as essential elements of day-to-day living.

Work

Work offers wonderful opportunities for self-expression. No longer is it a place to satisfy one's ego and hide one's insecurities. Work is growing in importance for the Young Adults especially because it adds to their understanding of how the world works.

Self-Esteem

The compulsive Adolescent need for constant praise and reinforcement is gone. Taking its place is the confidence of knowing one's value and worth. This allows the YA to spend less time worrying and struggling and more time learning and growing.

Problems

Problems are opportunities for Young Adults. No longer worried about who is to blame, they focus on what is causing a problem and how to go about fixing it. They are becoming masterful at finding the root cause of problems and crafting solutions that will last. Short-term fixes don't impress them.

FAMILY

Family is now a central part of the lives and futures of Young Adults. They are working to resolve tensions or breakdowns in family relationships and looking for ways to enrich and expand those relationships. They recognize the critical role families can play in their lives.

STRESS

Relieved of the need to avoid being blamed when something goes wrong, Young Adults are noticeably more calm and clear-thinking under stress. Where they once might have panicked, they now become focused — providing a sense of certainty and stability in the midst of chaos.

RESPONSIBILITY

There is a shift toward willingness to take responsibility for their actions. Young Adults care about outcomes but they do not try to duck their role when the outcomes are not what everyone desired. YAs now worry less about consequences and more about how to fix problems to which they may have contributed.

Tony's Story: Part Three
A Stumble, then Breakthrough

Tony was now determined to move up in the management ranks and earn some real money. And he did. Within two years, he was a regional manager. Two and a half years later, he became a vice president. His base salary had tripled, compared to what he had been making as customer service manager, and he was given stock options for the first time.

But as the years passed, Tony felt like he had hit another plateau. He seemed unable to move beyond vice president. He started getting antsy. He had a vague sense that he was losing control of things. A mentor might have helped, but he had long since lost contact with his friend Kim, and no one had appeared to fill that role.

Then Tony was summoned to the CEO's office. He wondered if he was going be chewed out for something. Maybe the CEO had heard about that ugly scene with another manager last week, right in front of the staff. He paused outside the executive suite, put on his "best face" and then entered. He looked friendly and confident, but sweat was trickling down his back as he shook hands with the CEO. After a few moments of small talk, Tony began to relax. But then the CEO turned serious. "Tony," he said, "I want you to see a counselor, at our expense. Your behavior, especially your hostility, has everyone in the organization upset. Nobody wants to work with you. You need to get to the root of whatever is bothering you."

Tony was stunned. He had no idea that his colleagues felt this way about him. After all, he had taken great pains to develop an image that was professional and competent. What could the CEO be talking about?

The counseling sessions were his first experience with any kind of therapy. He had never read a self-help book and had no familiarity with psychology or human behavior studies. So it was not surprising that he got off to a rocky start, especially when pressed to experience emotions that he had never acknowledged or talk about feelings without throwing a tantrum. But over a period of several months, at times on the verge of quitting, Tony started to break through. His compulsion to protect his image at all costs began to lessen. Old, almost forgotten feelings of curiosity about life and learning began to resurface. He felt more compassionate, more genuine.

Tony's life began to change in virtually every way. His relationship with his ex-wife and his children improved. Full of enthusiasm, he told his high school buddies about his experience, including the counseling. But all they did was make fun of him or change the subject. At a weekend barbecue, where he was kidded loudly about "seeing a shrink," he had a profound realization. The hurt that he felt from their put-downs was the same hurt that he had been inflicting on his colleagues at work. He felt shame and remorse as the thought sank in

— he had been so cruel and manipulative to others. He left the barbecue promising himself that he would never treat people that way again.

Soon he lost interest in hanging out with his beer-drinking buddies and became more drawn to people he could learn from, people he could admire.

(To be continued)

The Maturity Factor

6

THE WISE ADULT

B ill was an avid student of organizational effectiveness. So he naturally was eager to get started on his new assignment: to head a team of executives planning the spin-off of one of his company's divisions. The new organization's cultural values would be liberating, free of the "remnants of darkness" that hobbled the parent company, as Bill put it. He and his colleagues would create a management philosophy that was open to learning, resistant to bureaucracy and prepared to reward initiative at all levels.

I was brought in to work with Bill and the team, and I was immediately impressed with his maturity. He made sure everyone had a chance to participate in work sessions and was open to new ideas, even when they were counter to his own. It was clear that all he wanted was to make this new organization more effective. When he critiqued the parent company, there was no finger-pointing or resentment. His comments were matter-of-fact, intended to stimulate thinking about how to do it better. He made the work sessions a sort of laboratory in which the team could learn from past mistakes and create a more innovative organization that did a better job of managing its people — in other words, a wiser, *more effective* organization.

It also helped that Bill had a great sense of humor. So while he was quite adamant about the cultural values he wanted to implant in this "baby" they were giving birth to, he was also lighthearted enough that team members actually looked forward to each day's work.

At dinner with Bill several months later, I got a glimpse of his well-rounded personal life and saw it as yet another reflection of the confident and well-adjusted person I knew from our team-building exercises. This was a man who possessed greater wisdom and maturity than most people far older than he. Clearly, Bill was a Wise Adult. And he was only twenty-seven!

Bill went on to become a top executive in the new company. I often heard him referred to as the new company's "soul," an acknowledgment of his role as steward of the company's lifeforce. The last I heard, Bill had been promoted to chief executive officer, was a respected figure in his industry, and was enjoying fatherhood with a wonderful family. And he was still under 35.

PROFILE OF THE WISE ADULT:

➤ Has grown into full adulthood and enjoys it.

➤ Is confident of his or her identity and self-esteem; no longer obsesses either.

➤ Has a healthy perspective when it comes to relating to the rest of the world.

➤ Thirsts for knowledge; has a strong desire to learn and grow.

➤ Pursues self-improvement; wants to be more effective in all areas of life.

➤ Possesses an authentic enthusiasm for work and life.

➤ Knows how things work.

MAKING THINGS WORK

The Wise Adult (WA) is a person no longer in transition. Wise Adults have maneuvered successfully through the narrows of their youth, survived adolescence with minimal difficulty, and found themselves finally in full-fledged adulthood. Managers who are WAs think and act from a deeply rooted and well-tested maturity. Because they are comfortable with who they are, they see themselves more clearly than most of us. They are clear about their values and morals. They operate from an optimistic point of view and trust that everything is purposeful. They focus on how to make things work.

WA managers inspire personal growth and intellectual excitement in others just by their presence. When Wise Adults get together, you can count on it being a stimulating and pleasurable event.

Their wisdom resides not in the amount of information that they possess, or even the amount of education which they have acquired. Rather it is how they use the education, experience and intelligence that they have.

Their relationships at work and in their personal lives reflect an understanding of genuine partnership. They find joy in continuously learning and growing. Making a contribution to the larger society is an essential element in their lives. WAs frequently do volunteer work and are often the most generous philanthropists, donating millions to chosen universities and other causes.

WAs seldom visit the Adolescent domains; they are emotionally "grounded," free of the haunting fears that so frequently overwhelm Adolescents. They trust their friends and they trust themselves. Importantly, they trust the future.

THE "S-WORD"

I feel the need to make a distinction between spirituality and religion here. Many, many people shy away from any mention of the "S-word" because of their childhood experiences with religion. But the confusion is certainly not limited to those who've been burned or disillusioned in the past. So the field is quite muddy, even among the sophisticated. A colleague of mine, business philosopher and futurist John Renesch, writes in his book, *Getting to the Better Future: A Matter of Conscious Choosing*, that "Spirituality serves as a context for interconnectedness with those parts of ourselves that are not necessarily material or physical. It is formless. It contains no specific content or dogma. It allows for a direct relationship with the Divine through one's personal experience."

Renesch describes religion as being "based on specific concepts or form in which spirituality is viewed. It contains beliefs, rules, structure and, very often, tradition. It takes many forms, usually based upon the teachings of an enlightened being such as a prophet or someone else who is seen as having a very special relationship with the Divine."

The Dalai Lama explains the difference between religion and spirituality in his book *Ethics for a New Millennium*. He defines religion as "claims to salvation of one faith or another." He states that spirituality is expressed through certain "qualities of the human spirit – such as love and compassion, patience, tolerance, forgiveness, contentment, a sense of responsibility, a sense of harmony."

Further, he writes, "Religion is something we can perhaps do without. What we can't do without are those basic spiritual qualities."

SPIRITUAL PRINCIPLES

In my own process I have discovered the following spiritual principles that seem to always be part of life:

> *Connection: we're all in this together, connected in some seen or unseen way.*

> *Spirit is Real: whether it's called Higher Power or Spirit or God or Goddess or "All That Is" or Nature, this force is as real as I let it be in my life; it has the power and quality of magic and elegance.*

> ➤ *Elegant Unfolding: all problems and upsets, breakdowns, etc. (the death of my stepson Brad) are part of an elegantly unfolding future.*

> ➤ *Willingness: my learning and growth as a spiritual being is a function of how willing I am to fully experience life on life's terms and not lose myself to one event or one emotion.*

I know many TAs and HFAs who claim to be very religious but they relate to religion mostly through the Adolescent set of views and needs that they have. For instance, an Adolescent would likely see religion as a set of rules, dogma, or a structured way to live. So, for them, "following the rules" means acting religiously, which often translates to being "good," which unfortunately often translates further into "I'm better than you are."

Oftentimes, Adolescents will rebel against their religion and break the "rules" they perceive as having power over them. It is my experience that this rebellion is as much a part of adolescence as looking good is. Rebellion goes with the territory when you feel dominated or forced into a set of mores like the rules of that religion the way the Adolescent sees it.

It is not uncommon for a person to have a "spiritual awakening" from a significantly traumatic event and for a dramatic shift in their maturity to take place. Professional bicycle racer Lance Armstrong almost lost his life to cancer but found something within himself that was more powerful and expressive than the power of cellular biological operating principles. His successive Tour de France victories in 1999, 2000, 2001 and 2002, after coming back from cancer, inspired millions who watched in awe at this young man whose inner commitment was stronger than the biology.

The Wise Adult concept of spirituality also sets them apart from Adolescents. WAs see themselves as part of something larger — something powerful and humbling all at once. They derive satisfaction from spiritual relationships that are inclusive and generous. Adolescents, on the other hand, tend to become self-righteous about their belief systems, thus excluding others, or they use religion as a pretense to gain acceptability.

Wise Adults generally understand that there are four essential elements when it comes to being human: mind, body, spirit and emotions. No single one of these can dominate; each must receive equal attention. I think of them as a "quadrinity" of sorts. Sometimes the WAs' understanding of this is conscious and sometimes it is intuitive, but in either case they usually manage to integrate the four elements into both their work and personal lives.

This is a more remarkable achievement than it may seem.

We in the West have grown accustomed to the presence of only two of these at work - the mind and the body. We tend to leave the emotions and spirit at home. The reasons are obvious. Emotions are too complex, too uncontrollable, too "sticky." Spirit, because it is the element that includes (but is not limited to) religious beliefs, is filled with the potential for conflict. After all, aren't most wars due to religious differences and who has God on their side?

The sad fact is that most people bring only half of themselves to work - their bodies and minds. It's as if they believe they can turn their emotions and spirits down to the pilot-light level when they go to work and turn them back up at home. Over time, however, they even forget how to do this. They soon find themselves trapped in a life marked by struggle and pain — denied the opportunity to grow in a balanced way and cut off from the full experience of being one's true self.

Wise Adults can sense when the relationship between the elements is beginning to tumble out of balance. They act quickly to repair the damage and then reintegrate the four elements back into their lives.

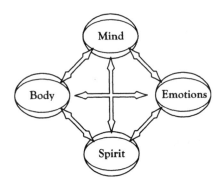

RITES OF PASSAGE

Making the leap from Young Adult to Wise Adult is a different process for each person. But there are some common signposts along the way.

INTROSPECTION

At some point in their lives, YAs begin to feel a need to better understand what they are all about. How energetically they act on that feeling has a lot to do with their transition into Wise Adulthood. For learning how to be introspective – to uncover and explore one's deepest feelings, emotions and thoughts – is critical to becoming a WA. It is key to sustaining the momentum of personal growth, the essence of Wise Adulthood. Without mastering the skill of introspection, no one can expect to find his or her place in the larger society.

FEEDBACK AND COACHING

YAs are still getting used to the idea of asking someone to coach them or provide feedback and maybe trying it out. But Wise Adults know they *need* both, that coaching and feedback are central to personal and professional success. WAs seek out informed and trustworthy people who can help them better understand themselves or introduce them to new information or both. They don't let their egos get in the way of listening to someone who has a valid opinion or useful perspective to offer. And they are discerning enough to know to whom they should listen and when.

NEUTRALITY/WITNESS

Virtually every Wise Adult has discovered a very magical skill that I call "neutrality" or "witness" — the ability to view a person or object or event without feeling any particular reaction. Imagine curiosity tempered by dispassion. (The Zen concept of "beginner's mind" is similar.) When WAs practice this skill, they let go of preconceived thoughts or emotional "baggage" that might cloud their vision. They become almost like disinterested bystanders, able to weigh what they are witnessing without becoming emotionally involved. The payoff for WAs is being able to see things as they really are. Imagine watching a minor car accident in slow motion. If you had the proper perspective and were not related to the parties involved, you could see what most people could not see — what actually happened. Wise Adults are in search of what is actually happening, not what they or other people think is happening. They know that true power in life lies in knowing how things really are.

Confronting Powerlessness

All of us have moments in our lives when we feel powerless to control events. In my own life, I felt it most directly when a ten-year-old friend of mine died without warning. Talk about powerlessness! The question is not *will you have such moments,* but *how will you react?* when they do occur.

Wise Adults have waded through these difficult currents and emerged with an understanding that eludes most of us: *When you feel powerless, don't fight it. Give up the idea that you are in charge, that you can manage the outcome of an event. Paradoxically, you can only regain your balance by abandoning all expectations of controlling the uncontrollable.* This is an essential life lesson for all of us. But only the WAs understand that they can expand their power by first surrendering. And they know *when* to let go and *how* to let go. This insight is wasted on Low Functioning Adolescents, for whom surrender to anything is not an option. And for High Functioning Adolescents, it becomes little more than something to spout at twelve-step meetings or training sessions. But Young Adults are likely beginning to experiment with the concept. If they follow the example of the Wise Adult, they will learn that each moment of powerlessness is a rite of passage on the path to self-mastery.

PASSING THE WISE ADULT TEST

Wise Adults have a very different view of what it means to be alive. They are intent on making the most of their time on earth. They thirst for the essence of life and pursue it in a deliberate but thoughtful way. Their ultimate goal: a life that has symmetry, that is in balance.

Carline's experience is a good example of this. I met her when she was a 32-year-old mid-level manager at a high technology enterprise. She and her husband and three children lived in Wichita, Kansas, close to her parents and in-laws but far from the parent company's headquarters in Washington, D.C.

And therein lay the problem. The company wanted a closer look at Carline to see if she was ready to move up the executive ladder, and so it offered her a special project to run at the headquarters office. The offer came with a promotion and a promise that she could return home to Kansas in 12 to 18 months, after the project ended.

Carline, already a respected manager, said yes and moved herself and her family to a temporary residence in Washington. My firm was hired to work with her on the project, the goal of which was to reduce the time it took to move the company's products into the marketplace. I knew that if she succeeded, she would be under pressure to join the corporate staff, no matter what promises had been made about returning to Kansas. I also knew, as did she, that nobody could advance to the highest levels of management in that company without living and working in Washington.

When I suggested she might face a tough decision at the end of her assignment, she laughed and told me not to worry. She had absolutely no intention of remaining in the East, she insisted. Her life with her extended family in Kansas was too important. This, I thought to myself, will be a real test of her adulthood.

I soon learned that what Carline wants, Carline gets. In fact, I had originally thought she might be a High Functioning Adolescent because of her excitement and energy. But after I saw how she kept focused on the future and always searched for the best way to accomplish a task, I revised my assessment to Young Adult. She quickly assembled an extraordinary team of people from all over the world to work with her and began to exhibit the kind of wisdom and thoughtfulness that is the hallmark of Wise Adults. When she trusted someone, she always asked for coaching and input. No matter what demands were put on her, Carline kept a firm grip on her values and a clear vision of what she wanted.

As you might imagine, she was quite successful and the High Functioning Adolescents who ran the headquarters office wanted to claim her as their own. (Behaving like most HFAs, they wanted credit for having made such a wise decision to promote her and put her on this critical project.) They pressed her to take another promotion and to stay in Washington longer.

Carline called me. She was calm and collected but wanted to bounce her thoughts off a disinterested observer. She told me how she had made a promise to her family and that she was intending to keep it. But did I think she was assigning too much importance to her family's desires? I laughed and told her I had nothing to offer but my admiration and support.

Carline took her husband and children back to Wichita. The company was smart enough not to punish her for her decision and returned her to its Kansas management group. There was no promotion, but that was of secondary importance for Carline. Her inner well-being and her family's happiness were more important than making more money. It was a Wise Adult decision.

A Wise Woman and Her Husband

The first person I ever met who fit my definition of Wise Adult was Buckminster "Bucky" Fuller, inventor of the geodesic dome, philosopher and world citizen. He came to Berkeley, California, for a lecture in the late 1970s; I was working with the sponsoring organization and had been asked to escort his wife for the day. She was in her late 70s or early 80s at the time, yet filled with youthful excitement. We sat together in the audience, close to the front so Bucky could see her from the stage.

When he began speaking, I was totally enthralled. I knew I was in the presence of genius, although I could understand only some of what he was actually saying. Bucky spoke in metaphors and similes and wound them around concepts, abstractions and principles that totally eluded me. But I knew something wonderful was happening and everyone in the audience sensed it, too.

After an hour and a half, it was time for intermission. I turned to ask Mrs. Fuller if I could do anything for her. She was slumped over, sleeping like a baby, snoring ever so softly. As the audience milled about, I sat there frozen. Do I awaken the wife of one of the most brilliant thinkers of our time and, by so doing, upset her? Or do I let her sleep and miss the bathroom break that she might later wish she had taken? It was a terrible quandary for me. Suddenly, the noise in the auditorium awakened her. She smiled sweetly and I was profoundly relieved.

"So, you must be tired from your difficult travel schedule with your husband," I said.

She smiled again and said, "No, dear, actually I always sleep while Bucky's talking. I never have the slightest idea what he's talking about."

I was shocked. "But you sit here anyway?" I questioned.

"Of course," she told me. "We've been married for over fifty years and I know it makes him happy."

Years later, I realized I had been in the presence of *two* Wise Adults – Bucky *and* his wife. They were extraordinary people who made everyone feel so comfortable in their presence. The memory of that day is a reminder of how we must cherish those who are Wise Adults.

THE EVOLUTION OF A WISE ADULT MANAGER:

TIME

WAs have learned how to live in the present with vigor and clarity, understanding that life is fragile. At the same time, they have a healthy outlook on the future, a sense of well-being going forward. They are able to balance short-term needs against what is best for the long-term.

RELATIONSHIPS

Wise Adults know that functional relationships, based on information, freedom and self-expression, are critical. They have all but eliminated Adolescents from their circle of acquaintances, choosing rather to spend their precious time with other Adults.

EMOTIONS

The core emotion for a Wise Adult is joy! List the synonyms for joy and you have described the foundation that supports their emotional good health: delight, happiness, rapture, ecstasy, rejoicing, gratitude.

VALUES

WAs have fully developed standards of ethical conduct and behavior. These standards are the basis of their way of life – the guiding principles for every thought and action.

Because they shun situational ethics, they have the freedom to think and act and explore without constraint.

WORK

At work, Wise Adults are always looking for the greater good. Their solid ethics mean they will look askance at the expeditious decisions which HFAs regularly make to meet personal needs. WAs are a pleasure to work with or for, since they value partnership and are unimpressed by status.

SELF-ESTEEM

No longer obsessed by worries over self-worth, Wise Adults live in a world in which self-esteem is a non-issue. Rather, they are constantly striving to grow and evolve, to become better citizens and better role-models. They have an uncanny ability to observe and evaluate their own behaviors without feeling impelled to pass judgment on themselves.

PROBLEM SOLVING

WAs are able to focus on short- and long-term problems and solutions. That makes them an organization's best resources for continuity and expansion. WAs can see existing or potential problems that Adolescents around them are causing or ignoring, an ability that protects their companies from legal action or customer catastrophes.

FAMILY

WAs usually shine in family relationships. They have the will and commitment to find balance for themselves and their family members. Because of their values, they will not sacrifice family happiness and emotional well-being to satisfy their career ambitions.

STRESS

Like eagles sitting atop trees in a forest, WAs have developed the capacity and patience to observe without overreacting. They are willing to act when it is necessary to do so but have tremendous patience and the ability to choose the right moment to step into a situation.

TONY'S STORY: CONCLUSION
PAIN, HEALING AND REWARDS

Tony's competence as an executive grew enormously, and he was soon promoted to senior vice president. *How did I ever waste so many years trying to keep up appearances when simply living life and being who you are is so much fun,* he mused to a friend.

He remarried a woman who had two children herself. Now he was a stepfather of pre-teens, even while his two boys were in college. But he was able to finance their tuition and had an amicable relationship with their mother, who had also happily remarried. Tony realized now that his own immaturity probably had much to do with the failure of his first marriage, though he couldn't see it at the time.

Then, just when everything was looking so sunny, tragedy struck in Tony's life. His wife's youngest child, eight-year-old Alisa, drowned during a family vacation after falling from the raft they were riding down a Colorado river. It was a fluke accident and no one was really to blame. But the loss was devastating to her mother and to Tony, who had grown quite attached to the youngster.

The impact of Alisa's death was so incapacitating that Tony and his family entered grief counseling, together in some sessions and individually at other times. The experience reminded him of the benefits he had received from counseling many years earlier at his CEO's insistence, and he decided to continue with regular therapy. Now Tony was looking beyond the healing process and toward greater personal growth. He committed himself to a life of self-examination, as he called it, and told a friend that it was a gift from Alisa.

Three years after the accident, Tony had recovered his emotional bearings. His family ties were stronger than ever. He was recruited to be the CEO of a technology company spin-off, the deal sweetened by a handsome signing bonus and generous compensation package. He left his old company in good standing and remained friendly with the CEO who, thankfully, had intervened in Tony's life years earlier.

Tony had made the full journey, from Low Functioning Adolescent to High Functioning Adolescent to Young Adult to Wise Adult. His experience proves that people can travel the road to Adulthood at any time in their lives. Getting started just requires a willingness to grow. Life will provide everything else.

7

ADOLESCENTS AND ADULTS TOGETHER

I t's the end of the day and I'm resting in my hotel room. I've just finished working with twenty middle and upper level managers at a large telecommunications company. I mentally replay the day's highlights as I relax.

Not surprisingly, it was a mixed group. Several of them were solid, committed individuals who were always looking for the win. They wanted what was best for the business. Lori, a 34-year-old middle manager, was typical — a clear thinker, fearless, compassionate, focused on people. If you didn't know her age, you'd think you were speaking to someone much older and more experienced. On the job, she calmly juggled complex problems and a constant stream of calls from clients and colleagues without missing a beat. I put her down as a Young Adult.

Four or five of the participants also caught my immediate attention, but for all the wrong reasons. They looked frustrated and downtrodden. Even the ones with seniority wore their unhappy emotions on their sleeves. I put them down as Adolescents (mostly HFAs, I guessed) and prepared myself for the predictable tensions between them and Lori and her Adult colleagues.

Tom, one of the gloomy ones, particularly interested me. A 24-year veteran of the telecommunications field, he was respected by everyone for his expertise and technical skills. When he was not being challenged, he was friendly enough. But if someone disagreed with him or he thought he was under attack, he lashed out with nasty, belittling comments. His manner became rash, harsh, edgy and judgmental. He was unmistakably a High Functioning Adolescent.

In our session that day, Lori and Tom quickly became embattled. The issue was a commitment that Tom had made the week before, but failed to keep. Lori, speaking in a straightforward manner, simply wanted him to acknowledge what he had done.

Tom got angry, then defensive, then accusatory. He tried blaming Lori and her team for failing to perform in other, unrelated situations. But Lori remained cool and, in the end, prevailed. She did so by always keeping the real issue in sight and refusing to take Tom's remarks personally.

It was a fascinating demonstration of the kind of encounters to expect when the management of a company is in the hands of both Adults and Adolescents.

BE READY FOR ANYTHING

When newcomers join a company's management ranks, all the existing managers naturally size them up. The LFAs and the HFAs in particular are anxious to know if any of the new arrivals might be Adolescent allies. LFAs and HFAs have a real knack for this. It is much like the alcoholic who can distinguish between social drinkers and other alcoholics at a bar or party. LFAs and HFAs somehow find each other, and very quickly. Often, they rally around a common interest, like sports, or a higher-level executive who is just like them. The LFAs and HFAs are driven by the need to be with people who will make them feel good about themselves, who will validate them in some way. This means someone who finds them funny or interesting or unusual, or who exudes sexual energy or tension.

But the most interesting thing to watch is the inevitable attacks that Adolescent managers of either stripe will mount against newly arrived Young Adults. Like vultures circling over small animals on the desert floor, they hover poised and ready to attack. They snicker among themselves and watch to see which YAs seem most vulnerable. The predictable actions that Adolescents take in executing these attacks are:

➤ *Belittling the YAs in front of other managers in hopes of undermining their credibility and diminishing their influence.*

➤ *Trying to persuade the YAs to buy into the Adolescent perspective of reality and, in the process, sabotage the still-developing maturity of the YAs.*

➤ *Spreading gossip about the YAs among other managers or subordinates.*

➤ *Provoking arguments with the YAs in hopes of knocking them off balance emotionally.*

Young Adult managers sometimes succumb briefly to one or more of these tactics. Because they are young and still evolving, they can be influenced if the Adolescents are persistent. But sooner or later, the YAs' internal guidance system of values and ethics usually prompts course corrections. They end up working harder, communicating more intensely or simply finding new ways to solve problems.

I saw this happen with Adelle, whom I met in a workshop for new supervisors at a West Coast biotechnology company. She was bright, friendly and easy to be around, a thirty-year-old emerging Young Adult with some lingering Adolescent traits. Recently divorced, she was prone to occasional caustic outbursts about her ex-husband. And she could be impulsive at times; once she took her two-year-old automobile in for a tune-up and ended up buying a new car on the spur of the moment.

But I attributed such behaviors to the fact that she was still working her way into Adulthood, and I was especially impressed with her depth of character. When a friend was diagnosed with cancer, Adelle rallied co-workers and acquaintances and organized an event at which everyone could express support for their stricken comrade. And she did it without seeking recognition or praise.

Her claim to the rank of Young Adult was amply demonstrated when the company teamed her and another manager together on a project. He was a High Functioning Adolescent, and the combination of these two intelligent and determined people could have been explosive. The HFA tried hard to manipulate her so that he could gain greater control and, in the end, get most of the credit for the project's success.

Adelle came to me with the problem and described how she intended to deal with it. Her thinking was sound and all I could add were a few comments about the way her strategy might play out. A few months later, she sent me an e-mail update. She had handled the situation perfectly, with good results. But what impressed me was the thought she had put into her e-mail. Here is the ground she covered:

> ➤ *What happened.*

> ➤ *How the other manager reacted.*

> ➤ *Which of her actions showed that she had improved as a manager.*

> ➤ *What skills or behaviors she still needed to polish.*

> ➤ *What she had learned from the experience.*

> ➤ *How my input had helped her.*

> ➤ *And, thanks for my time!*

Seldom does an Adolescent of any kind report their learning experiences with that kind of depth and clarity. Yes, HFAs will tell you that they're learning. But that usually means they are trying to make a good impression, rather than actually coming to grips with the way they think and act. Adelle was clearly showing me that she was integrating her new insights into her approach to management. In the process, she was mastering Young Adulthood.

PROBLEM SOLVING
VS. POUTING

Put a tough challenge before a group of Adult and Adolescent managers and watch how differently each responds. The Adults turn their attention to the matter at hand and look for solutions. The Adolescents immediately feel under attack and look for ways to defend themselves. High Functioning Adolescents in particular try to redirect everyone's attention away from the real issues and shift the "blame" to someone else.

I watched this very scene develop at a client company where the management team had gathered to hear a message from their boss. The message was simple: while the team seemed to think that all was well, the company actually had a crisis on its hands. When was the team going to recognize that the crisis existed and react appropriately?

The Adults listened carefully to what was being said and appeared to be taking their boss at her word. But the HFAs seemed annoyed and distant, even offended. One of them, Joan, finally spoke up. Things weren't as bad as they seemed, she said with obvious disdain. Her manner was so self-righteous and jarring that it instantly changed the tone of the meeting — disorienting everyone for a moment and throwing the discussion off track.

Fred, an Adult, quickly jumped in with remarks that steered the group back to the question posed by the boss. This is what Adults do. They keep everyone focused on the real issues and dealing with them.

The HFAs fell silent. When the meeting ended, I wondered if any of them had even the slightest insight into how unhelpful they had been. The next day, I asked each of the managers this simple question: "What behaviors and actions do you need to change, adapt, or shift in *yourself* today during the meeting to expand the group's effectiveness?"

From the Adults came comments like:

"Be more concise and stay focused."

"Help facilitate the group's movement when things bog down."

"Not repeat myself when I don't get the reaction that I want in the group."

The HFAs were quiet, clearly unwilling to risk exposing any weakness or assume any fault for their behavior. Finally, I put a question to one of them.

"What happened with you yesterday?" I asked. "You

didn't seem to participate at all."

She gave me the proverbial look that could kill. I could tell she was upset at being singled out, though her lack of participation had been obvious to everyone.

She mustered up a fake smile. Then, harkening back to an earlier discussion about the need to be good listeners, she said sweetly: "I was practicing 'listening.'" There was an unspoken "screw you" in her reply.

After the session, I told the Adults that they needed to step up and take more responsibility for the quality of the sessions. They did just that, and the team began making real progress.

The Adolescents found themselves in retreat. One of them, a severe example of a Low Functioning Adolescent, declared that he was ill and needed to go home. It was the only way he knew to cope with the situation. He was a perpetually angry man who often yelled to get what he wanted; he had two legal actions pending against him, both filed by co-workers. As I watched him leave, I thought it might be in the cards for this man to leave the team, perhaps even leave the organization. His other choice, of course, was to start growing up.

Pressure Handled Differently

Adolescent managers of all stripes often cut and run when they fear that they will be exposed for who they are. I recall, for example, an HFA manager at a client company who seemed determined to make herself look good at the expense of colleagues. While they listened in some dismay, she made exaggerated claims of success for her division and boasted that her results were the "best in the company."

But her bravado did not impress the executive who was presiding over the meeting. He kept pressing her to support her assertions, one after another, and she kept falling short. Soon she seemed to be losing her confidence; her manner became less certain.

She looked to her "friends," the other HFAs, for sympathy but got none. By now, they were visibly upset with her; they worried that her sorry performance might make the boss start questioning everybody. She was trapped in a web of deception that she had created for herself. Each time she intimated that her successes far outpaced those of her fellow managers, her boss pressed her for evidence. Before long, she became openly confused, then fearful and panicked.

The room fell silent as the exchange between her and her boss became more pointed. Suddenly, she stood up, looked at him, and said, "I'm sorry, but I've been getting a migraine headache for the last hour. I need to get some medication and take a break." She left the room at warp speed. Everyone knew what had happened. There was nothing left to say. The adults looked at each other knowingly. The HFAs, by now totally paranoid, looked at each other with fear and uncertainty.

Contrast the discredited manager's behavior with that of Jean, who began as a secretary for a Chicago-based technology company in her early twenties and worked her way up to a supervisorial job at the age of forty-five.

She was one of the firm's oldest "new" supervisors when I met her while conducting leadership training sessions. I was impressed by her personal ethics and determination. She had earned a college degree at the age of thirty-nine while working full-time. She exhibited the maturity of an older woman but the enthusiasm of a 30-something. As a new manager she was, according to her boss, a "dream."

But because of her age and her history as a secretary, Jean was often challenged by other newly arrived managers and even subordinates who thought she wasn't tough enough to be a supervisor. A lesser person might have folded under the pressure. But Jean quickly took charge, exhibiting firmness without alienating the most able members of her team.

She had a special way of describing her first encounters with under-performers. Those, she said with a smile, were "red dot moments." It was a couple of years before I connected her phrase to the red dot that a laser-sighting gun projects onto a target. In this case, the target was the employee's substandard performance. Jean's intense focus guaranteed that each of them, particularly the Adolescents, would get the message fast — either perform or face the consequences.

This is the kind of Young Adult manager that other Adults love to have working in a company. Jean is open to feedback, brings a positive attitude to the job and is a wonderful role-model for others of modest beginnings. And she is committed to her team members learning and growing together. Wouldn't every company love to have a few dozen Jeans in its management ranks?

WHAT A MANAGER CAN DO

By now, you may be wondering if any management team can be effective, given the likelihood that its members will run the gamut from Low Functioning Adolescent to Wise Adult. Diversity like that would seem to guarantee failure, or at least gridlock. The answer lies in how well the executive in charge, or the team leader, integrates the less mature people into the group's operations. Here are four guideposts to a successful outcome:

PATIENCE

The willingness to hang in there as participants who are less mature but have clear potential begin to show signs of emotional and mental growth. Calmness, endurance and commitment are essential. But patience should not get in the way of dealing decisively with those unable to develop quickly enough for the needs of the team.

CLEAR EXPECTATIONS

Making sure that the less mature know exactly what is expected of them. An easily understood definition of success is important. Desired behaviors should be spelled out. The targets in all cases should be relatively simple.

Consistency

No wavering when it comes to judging whether results meet expectations. Enforcement of goals must be consistent. Often, a leader invests so much energy working with a less mature team member that he or she is tempted to settle for something less than a successful performance. But in doing so, the leader may put the team results at risk.

Rewards And Consequences

A clear statement of the rewards that will follow if the team meets its goals vs. the consequences if it fails. Once success or failure is known, rewards or consequences must instantly follow. Without this quick linkage, the less mature team member may well miss the point. The worst error is to delay or avoid imposing consequences – a common management mistake.

8

WITHOUT ADULTS, A DYSFUNCTIONAL ORGANIZATION

Organizations whose management ranks are dominated by the less mature pay an unacceptably heavy price. Some of it can be calculated in dollars — for example, the cost to settle a sexual harassment lawsuit against a supervisor whose attitude toward women never got beyond that of a sixteen-year-old with raging hormones. Or the sudden rise in health insurance claims and sick days taken because unthinking managers have made the workplace so stressful for employees. Some of it is harder to measure: energy wasted on work assignments that have no purpose, operating inefficiencies, time spent waiting for others who are late to meetings, time wasted gossiping.

And how do you measure the truly intangible costs, especially the psychic burden borne by the unfortunate employees who are at the receiving end of Adolescent management practices. Let's also factor in what I think of as the cost to our souls — the dreams that go unfulfilled and the potential that is unrealized in the workforce because of less-than-mature management behavior. These are the sad results when managers fail to provide the support that employees need to achieve maximum performance and to experience the joy of knowing they produced the best possible results.

On those too-infrequent occasions when I visit a company that is blessed with more mature management, I am startled by the contrast. Every positive trait that you would wish an enterprise to exhibit is suddenly visible, from strong employee loyalty to intense focus upon customer needs. When later I find myself at an organization dominated by Adolescent managers, I am struck anew by their destructive impact. Suffice it to say that the cost of tolerating this immaturity is staggering. It affects:

> *Productivity at all levels.*

> *Workplace creativity.*

> *Organizational effectiveness and overall sustainability.*

> *Efficiency of operations.*

> *Customer satisfaction.*

> *Employee satisfaction.*

> *Shareholder value.*

> *A company's contribution to the community.*

➤ *Wise use of resources; sustaining the environment.*

➤ *Access to opportunities.*

➤ *Capacity to deal with change.*

➤ *Ability to adapt to competitive pressures.*

➤ *Survival in the world marketplace.*

It is no exaggeration to say that the greater the population of Adolescents in a company's management ranks, the more likely that company will be dysfunctional. Allowing a company to be managed by individuals who lack interpersonal skills and maturity is akin to organizational self-destruction.

HOW THE FOUR TYPES OF MANAGERS INFLUENCE ORGANIZATIONS

If the dominant managers are:	Then expect the organization to be a:
Low Functioning Adolescents	Dysfunctional Organization
High Functioning Adolescents	Transitional Organization
Young Adults	Learning Organization
Wise Adults	Conscious Organization

THE SYMPTOMS OF DYSFUNCTION

There is nothing complicated about the way Adolescent managers lead a company into a state of dysfunction. Gather enough of them together and they will form a community among themselves that simply overpowers anything in its way. As they gain a stranglehold on management of the company, their traits become the company's traits. Their dysfunctionality infects its culture, and the company then begins to display the same dysfunctional behavior.

What do I mean by "dysfunctional?" *Webster's* defines it as "impaired or abnormal functioning." Psychology has used the term to describe a behavior that is obsessed with saving face and keeping secrets. My notion of a dysfunctional organization is close to what Anne Wilson Schaef and Diane Fassel described in their book, *The Addictive Organization*, published in the 1980s. Their studies led them to organizations that "behave like addicts" and harbor compulsive behaviors of all sorts, especially workaholism. Not surprisingly, these organizations attracted people prone to the same crippling compulsions.

I have seen too many companies whose dysfunctional cultures are quite accepting of heavy drinking or ridiculously long hours at work — the "24/7" life-style. Their predictably Adolescent managers simply do not address such compulsions, as if by secret understanding. Just like dysfunctional families, these companies have unwritten rules that essentially say, "We don't talk about that here," or "We just pretend that isn't happening," or "Let's keep this inside the company, okay?"

Pretense, in fact, is a sure sign of a dysfunctional organization. Have you seen the Dilbert cartoon where the boss is telling Dilbert that everyone needs to work 18 hours a day to keep up with the competition? Dilbert says this will wear people out, create stress and chaos, and actually harm performance. He suggests that instead of actually requiring everyone to work 18 hours, the boss should just tell the competition that they're working these hours. This, Dilbert reasons, will cause the competition to panic and begin working 18 hour days (using the same logic as the boss) — thus wrecking their productivity and giving Dilbert's company a great competitive advantage.

A work environment thick with gossip is another indicator of dysfunction. When the water cooler chatter is mainly tearing down an absent colleague's reputation or chortling over the latest sexual affairs or tsk-tsking over someone's drinking problem, you can bet the organization has a problem.

I said earlier that at the heart of these dysfunctional companies there will always be a group of Adolescents. Now the truly bad news: Sometimes, it can even be the founder! When that is the case, you can be sure the company culture will be one where other Adolescents feel comfortable and act out all their disagreeable behaviors. The declared mission statement may be, "We are united and aligned behind the corporate vision and goals." But the real mission statement will be unspoken, something suitably Adolescent like, "We will all take care of each other and protect each other's image while we are together in this company."

LFAs: They Cause the Most Damage

It goes without saying that Low Functioning Adolescents are the greatest contributors to dysfunction in a company. Count on them to be disruptive, negative and a major barrier to organizational effectiveness, productivity and morale. Often, it's little stuff. LFAs in particular have an uncanny ability to come up with excuses that seem viable but really aren't. When a management meeting is delayed because they are late, it isn't their fault; there was "traffic" on the way to the office. In my experience, this is the grown-up version of "the dog ate my homework." More often than not, actions like delaying a meeting are subconscious attempts by LFAs to control their environment and the people around them.

Low Functioning Adolescents tend to sit near each other in these meetings. They often engage in side conversations or quietly snicker about anything said that they disagree with or find offensive. They may exchange glances, looks and expressions, all of which are clearly intended to set them apart from everyone else. They enjoy the "inside joke" of it all.

Their tendency to flock together has its roots in a collective instinct to protect themselves against those who are seen as threats – their more mature co-workers. On a less-than-conscious level, the LFA managers put more importance on this than they do on achieving a company objective or project result. The irony is that relationships with LFAs are always tenuous, changeable and at the whim of their emotional and psychological needs.

The short attention spans of the Low Functioning Adolescents make them quite frustrating to work with and be with. Unless they find something so totally compelling as to absorb their entire consciousness, they tend to dart from one subject to another in the space of a moment. Traits like this put a heavy burden on the executive who must oversee the work of LFA managers; extraordinary doses of personal and professional attention are required.

Because of their immaturity, LFAs often do stupid things and create dangerous situations at work. They will ignore quality principles in their rush to get to an end result, without concern for the problems that might create. They cannot comprehend how their behavior is troublesome to others. From their perspective, they are managing in a perfectly normal and logical fashion, yet continue to find themselves swamped by problems and breakdowns. Not surprisingly, they feel like victims or martyrs. They live life with so much attention upon themselves that the long-term consequences of their actions evade them.

Consider the following actual incidents involving LFAs in the workplace:

> *A first level supervisor publicly rewards his four female employees with a dozen roses and an aluminum foil model of a twelve-inch penis, laughing as he hands each one out. Since his name is Ed, he calls the floral arrangements the "Ed Junior Award." He is terminated the next day.*

➤ *An employee receives an e-mailed pornographic picture from a friend. He forwards it to 35 of his fellow workers, but with one twist — he pastes his boss's face upon one of the people in the picture. He is fired the next day.*

The presence of an LFA manager in a company is not unlike having a terrorist bomb hidden on the premises. Only the terrorist knows when it is set to go off and what will cause it to explode. And there is no device a company can place at its entrance to detect this destructive force and keep it out of the building.

HFAs: Threats in Disguise

High Functioning Adolescents behave a lot like their LFA cousins but also create their own, more subtle, kind of dysfunction in an organization. They are especially threatening when they have hiring or promotion authority. They use their power to hire fellow HFAs, while excluding most others. In doing so, they create confusion and upset for anyone who is more mature.

HFA managers like to be firmly in command. When they sense they may be losing control to Adults, they quickly stir things up. Their frequent strategy is to regain control by throwing up a smokescreen of complexity and chaos. Just when the situation is at its worst, they stride to the rescue with a "solution" to the mess they in fact made. Naturally, they blame other people for causing the disruption. What they are really doing is positioning themselves to look good and claim credit for another managerial "success."

In an earlier chapter, I discussed how High Functioning Adolescent managers are not as clueless as the LFAs, how they have learned to function in the workplace *despite* their immaturity. But that ability can also make them more dangerous and can propel an organization more rapidly in the direction of dysfunction. Why? Because the competence of the HFAs can easily disguise their immaturity and mask its destructive effects. Adult colleagues may even be forgiving of their immaturity precisely because the HFAs are at least somewhat effective.

To the casual observer, High Functioning Adolescents may seem quite occupied with their work and always caught up in something important. But more likely, they are quietly looking for ways to expand their power. HFA managers are constantly lurking, constantly threatening, and constantly keeping things from working.

They especially add to dysfunction with their belief that causing people pain is the only way to get results or change behavior in the workplace. HFAs come to believe this because of the pain and/or suffering that they inwardly feel. Chances are they do not realize the damage they are doing. But it is an approach that comes naturally to them — pain deserves pain!

An organization dominated by HFA managers, or strongly influenced by them, can best be described as "being in transition." It is at a crossroad and can go either of two ways. It can evolve into the next level of organizational maturity — thus becoming more functional and effective — or it can *devolve* and regress, becoming totally dysfunctional.

WISE ADULTS TO THE RESCUE

In the end, it is the extent to which Adult managers are present and able to exert influence that determines whether a company will be functional.

If, for example, Young Adults are a major presence in management ranks, it is likely that company will become what Peter Senge described in his 1990 book, *The Fifth Discipline: The Art and Practice of The Learning Organization.* Because YAs are newly matured and eager to learn, they just naturally create an organizational culture that continuously seeks ways to grow and develop — the "learning organization" that Senge envisioned.

But it is the Wise Adult managers who have the greatest ability to propel a company along the path of functionality.

WAs tackle tough issues without becoming confused or overwhelmed. When a company is in crisis, having WA managers around is a great relief. The organization can count on them to act and behave in ways that empower the workforce and assure good results. Watch a Wise Adult manager in action and you will see:

➤ *A willingness to confront and engage the most difficult and complex issues.*

➤ *An attitude of acceptance, interest and even excitement when new problems arise.*

➤ *A focus not only on the immediate situation, but also on long-term implications.*

➤ *Actions that convey confidence and enthusiasm rather than fear, panic and doubt.*

➤ *An ability to keep calm even while others are on the verge of losing control.*

➤ *Strong perceptive skills, especially when it comes to seeing the patterns that underlie chaos and uncertainty.*

➤ *The know-how to bring the right people together to attack a* problem, then energize and focus them so that a constructive and timely solution emerges.

➤ An awareness that every event and outcome must be objectively observed and not taken personally.

➤ After the completion of a significant business undertaking, a focus on the lessons learned.

Wise Adult managers are blessed with a kind of self-correcting mechanism that allows them to take risks when the situation seems to warrant it, but also learn from their mistakes when they fail. Put another way, they take responsibility for their actions, no matter the results.

They may or may not relish paradox and complexity. But unlike Adolescents, WAs don't run from either or react with fear or terror; rather, their manner is deliberately matter-of-fact. They have the wisdom to know that it is futile to try and control such situations or to become hostile or to display any number of other Adolescent responses.

Charles Handy, the insightful author of *The Age of Paradox*, has written that "paradox does not have to be resolved, only managed." His work perfectly defines how Wise Adult managers look at paradox: "Paradox has to be accepted, coped with, and made sense of, in life, in work, in the community, and among nations." Expand the context to include complexity and chaos and you have a place where Wise Adults can flourish.

Imagine being on the battlefield, in an emergency room or in an intense business transaction. Who would you want managing one of those situations? Certainly not the Low Functioning Adolescents. They couldn't begin to sort out what needed to be done. And not the High Functioning Adolescents. They would have trouble seeing the full scope of the issues, much less the subtleties. The Young Adults would hang in there, but gaps in their experience could handicap them and their eagerness to engage the situation might blind them to its intricacies.

Only the Wise Adults would have the will, the experience and the clarity of judgment to handle the task with a high probability of success.

Dysfunctional organizations do a poor job of inspiring their workers, and I think it is because few, if any, Wise Adult managers are present. WAs bring what I would call a spiritual perspective to their jobs. They may not use this terminology; in fact, they would probably shun the word "spiritual," given the likelihood it would be confused with religiosity. But I have seen WA managers exhibit this larger perspective — a sort of "context of all contexts" that employees relate to, even if they can't explain why they do so. These managers reach people at the soul level. Their colleagues willingly follow their lead for reasons they often can't articulate.

The important truth is that Wise Adult managers can lift a company beyond mere operating efficiencies. They can take it to a level of organizational maturity that is "the polar opposite of dysfunctional," in the words of John Renesch. He coined the term "Conscious Organization" and it is a perfect description of the workplace environment that Wise Adults aspire to create.

In an article published in May, 2000, entitled "The Conscious Organization: Workplace for the Self-Actualized," Renesch described this most remarkable culture:

> *"It is not an end-state where every worker has been certified 'enlightened' and each and every element of the company, or division or bureau, or agency, or institution is spotlessly cleaned of any residual unconsciousness. The Conscious Organization is one which continually examines itself, committed to becoming as conscious as it can. In other words, it has very low tolerance for any unconsciousness. It possesses the collective will to be vigilant, the collective commitment to continuous evolution, and the collective courage to act."*

Once this Conscious Organization, or anyone involved with it, recognizes a quality, procedure, or other element of its culture that is not conscious, a rallying cry goes out and the organization's resources are marshaled toward "cleaning up" that area and making it more conscious. In this way it is the polar opposite of dysfunctional organizations.

Renesch, who developed his theory independent of my work, went on to explain the energy that creates Conscious Organizations and enables them to grow and prosper:

> *"Humanistic psychologist Abraham Maslow's Hierarchy of Needs declares that self-actualization is a state sought by all human beings once we have satisfied the more basic needs of survival, gratification and belonging.*
>
> *"It seems quite reasonable that as we humans continue to evolve and become more conscious beings there will be a concurrent need for our organizations to follow suit. As this becomes more widely recognized and people continue on their path of self-actualization, the enterprises, institutions and companies where human beings come together to produce results will need to change dramatically or die.*
>
> *"People in a Conscious Organization would be open to learning about any unwanted patterns and breaking through any barriers they may have. Having a conscious and healthy relationship with their co-workers and the organization's mission is of paramount importance, far more important than*

their need to maintain their image, the illusion of control, or remain in denial about something that violates their core values."

Doesn't this sound like the ideal culture for Wise Adults? Isn't this the type of organization that any Adult would want to work in? You bet!

9

Maturity Upgrading: Revitalizing Your Organization

Some colleagues have told me that they are not aware of ANY companies that are completely healthy — that is, fully functional. I'm not ready to make that claim, but I will say that I have not found many organizations meeting that high standard. My experience tells me that more organizations are dysfunctional than not, by a huge margin.

It is the short supply of Wise Adult managers that largely makes the difference. When I first developed my theory of the mature manager, I assumed there would be just as many Wise Adults out there as the other three management types, the LFAs, HFAs and YAs. But the Wise Adult population turned out to be the smallest of the four — not just small, but rare. I could count only a few hundred Wise Adults among the thousands of managers I had worked with over the past quarter century.

Grappling with this predicament requires an organization to do two things:

> ➤ *Identify managers who have clear potential to move up the maturity ladder, and then give them the help they need. I call the process "upgrading."*

> ➤ *Stop tolerating the presence of managers who will not or cannot grow into mature leaders. In most cases, this means summoning up the will to let them go.*

OUT OF THE MUD

METHODS OF UPGRADING

> ➤ Mentoring   ➤ Counseling
> ➤ Coaching   ➤ Severe Consequences

We're all familiar with upgrading as a computer-age term, meaning advancement to a higher level of functionality. When I apply it to people, I think of it as a way to get unstuck, like a car that finally is able to churn its way out of deep mud. For Adolescents, upgrading is moving toward Young Adulthood. For Young Adults, it means growing into Wise Adults. The maturation process that stalled somewhere in the past is revived. The inner forces that drive emotional and intellectual growth are reignited.

The concept is easy to describe, but how to put it into practice? I wrestled with this question for many months while conducting my research in the business world and observing management behavior. Here are the four upgrading techniques that I have found most effective:

MENTORING

The mentor must be a person able to provide non-judgmental feedback and role-modeling in a "safe" environment. Ideally, he or she will be an Adult who can show by example the more effective ways in which a manager can function. The best mentors will also encourage exploration of concepts such as "vision" and "values," neither of which LFAs and HFAs pay much attention to.

COACHING

Direct feedback is provided by a trusted peer or superior, or a consultant or other outsider. Coaches often require that specific actions or behaviors be undertaken, obliging managers who are being coached to execute the directives and report back. For that reason, coaching LFAs and HFAs will not succeed unless they commit to following instructions and growing from the experience.

INDIVIDUAL COUNSELING

Under the guidance of qualified professionals, this approach can enable persons to discover major traumas or other past life experiences that are causing or contributing to their stalled Adolescence. The goal is to overcome the blockages and allow the persons being counseled to regain their momentum toward maturity. Counseling can include psychotherapy. Once thought of as only applicable for "mentally ill" people, it is now widely utilized in personal and professional development for people who wish to grow and expand their knowledge of themselves.

SEVERE CONSEQUENCES

Demanding that Adolescent managers produce clear results or suffer explicit consequences is sometimes the only way to get their attention. It may jar them into a new state of personal awareness and restart the growth process — or it may send them running to find ways to escape. In such situations, organizations must be prepared to impose penalties for failure, up to and including termination.

Managers who turn away from opportunities to restart the growth process in themselves are ducking reality. But they cannot escape it forever. Worst of all, they will be ill-prepared to respond when reality does intrude in their lives. Something as simple as a speeding ticket at the worst possible moment in a hectic day will send them into an uncontrollable rage. An experience as painful as a life-threatening injury or the death of a loved one will simply crush their spirits.

Encounters with reality are "wake-up calls" that should not be ignored. Life is jolting us with an event that forces us to pay attention. The good news is that if we awaken from the first "call," we are likely to take what follows in stride. The bad news is that if we fail to awaken, the calls will get louder and the jolts may be much bigger.

Keep Pressing the LFAs

Methods of Upgrading

- ➤ Mentoring   ➤ Counseling
- ➤ Coaching   ➤ Severe Consequences

It will come as no surprise that Low Functioning Adolescents are the most resistant to upgrading. Again, it's not because they are bad people. They are simply not very functional. They are accustomed to "skating by" in most situations, doing their best to avoid accountability for their irresponsible and immature actions. They care mainly about getting away with as much as they can.

All of these factors make LFA managers prime candidates for the "severe consequences" approach: put the spotlight on them, press them for results, force them to keep communicating results or the lack thereof, and don't let them off the hook. The consequences for failure must be clearly stated at the outset and can include:

➤ *A reprimand and loss of face among colleagues.*

➤ *Public humiliation.*

➤ *Failure to be promoted.*

➤ *Demotion.*

➤ *Firing.*

When an organization puts this kind of heat on LFA managers, they will respond by (1) realizing that their behavior has been inappropriate and taking the first tentative steps toward improvement or (2) fleeing the scene as quickly as possible.

The counseling approach can be effective with LFAs, but in fewer instances. Similarly, LFAs can sometimes strike up a friendship with an Adult, out of which a coaching relationship evolves. But this is rare.

Most importantly, nothing can be done to help LFA managers mature unless they are willing to change. They must at some point demonstrate an openness to personal growth and a willingness to leave behind the artificial security of peer approval and image maintenance. No amount of senior managerial skill or attention will make a difference if the LFA manager refuses to participate.

I saw that in the case of Sonny, a fifty-something computer programmer who had worked for five different employers in six years. Married and divorced three times, he was the father of two children whom he rarely saw because they lived in a distant city. He had been forced to declare bankruptcy during his third marriage.

Sonny had minor management duties but performed them in such a lackluster manner that he was never a candidate for promotion. The situation had his employer stumped. Sonny hadn't done anything bad enough to be fired, his boss reasoned, but he wasn't pulling his weight. He was collecting his pay but putting forth little effort. The company asked me to meet with Sonny and see if I could help.

He struck me as a man chronically depressed, moping about and frequently emitting long sighs of self-pity. He liked to complain about his salary, which he thought insufficient. He rarely completed an assignment, but would accomplish enough of it to avoid criticism. He seldom asked questions about an assignment even if he was puzzled by aspects of it. His colleagues told me that even when he was smiling or laughing, they sensed that he would not extend himself to do a job well. Something was always left out or left undone.

After several sessions with Sonny, I was forced to conclude that he was stuck in his adolescence and had no desire to grow out of it. I recommended that the company discharge him at the next legal opportunity. This was a man far more committed to his mediocre level of work than to improving himself. The moral: *Sometimes managers simply don't want to grow and you have to part company with them.*

ODDS ARE BETTER WITH HFAS

LIKELY HFA UPGRADING SCENARIOS

Most likely:	Severe Consequences
Next most likely:	Counseling
Possible but less likely:	Mentoring
Least likely:	Coaching

Severe consequences are also the most likely prod to maturity for managers who are High Functioning Adolescents. Remember, HFAs are not necessarily more mature than LFAs, they are simply more skilled in certain areas. They have the same internal fixations and addictions as the LFAs and will cling to them just as strongly as the LFAs.

But HFAs are more susceptible to upgrading than LFAs. Indeed, the simple act of rubbing their faces in their own adolescence can force HFAs to recognize their immaturity for the first time and see the negative impact they have on others.

If the consequences are severe enough and lead to counseling, HFAs do have the capacity to respond. Some may even become enthusiastic about the process, once they have awakened to the promise of greater maturity.

Mentoring also can be effective in upgrading HFA managers, provided it is carried out in a nonthreatening manner. Done properly, mentoring can demonstrate to HFAs the wide gap between the way they do things and the way Adults function. The HFAs can emerge from this process with new and surprising personal insights.

Coaching offers much less certainty of success with HFAs. The technique can be a powerful tool because of the discipline it imposes. When personal coaches direct HFA managers to take specific actions or try to learn specific behaviors, the HFAs have no easy escape from what is being asked of them. But this can be tough for HFAs because their instinct is to interpret such directives as a direct assault on their ability and judgment.

As with the LFAs, upgrading will not happen unless the HFA managers are committed to changing, no matter what technique is employed. Their wholehearted enrollment is essential; they must want to grow.

YAs Are Eager Candidates

Likely YA Upgrading Scenarios

Most likely:	Mentoring
Next most likely:	Coaching
Then:	Counseling
Least Likely:	Severe Consequences

The upgrading process is just the opposite for Young Adult managers. Severe consequences are seldom needed to move YAs in the direction of Wise Adulthood. Instead, mentoring or coaching is the preferred technique; Young Adults thrive on either or both. The reason, of course, is their greater maturity. Unlike HFAs and LFAs, the Young Adults have already discovered the rewards of personal development and are quite open to the prospect of even more change and learning.

Also unlike the HFAs, Young Adult managers will almost always do well under skillful attention from upper management. If counseling is called for, most YAs will respond with willingness and even enthusiasm. This, too, is in striking contrast to the LFAs and HFAs, who generally submit to either only with reluctance and an air of resignation.

Since YAs are still relatively new to the ranks of Adulthood, some may relapse occasionally into Adolescence, especially if they spend much time with HFAs. Others may show a tendency to become quite comfortable, even lazy, now that they are Young Adults. This can be equally alarming. If they stop doing the homework needed to become a Wise Adult, the maturation process will grind to a stop. On occasions like these, the severe consequences approach might be needed. But since it's Young Adults we're dealing with, the recovery time should be short. What I like about YAs is their genuine interest in personal growth and their receptivity to mentoring and coaching. This attitude of openness makes them far more attractive to the Wise Adults, who are best positioned to help. What a contrast to the LFAs and HFAs, whose first impulse in most cases is resistance.

The receptivity of Young Adults to mentoring and coaching reminds me of my first experiences with golf. Trained as a ski instructor and being a competitive tennis player, I assumed golf would be easy to master. After all, the ball was just sitting there waiting to be hit! Of course, I quickly learned that the game was uncompromisingly complex and difficult.

Each day, I saw other less-than-accomplished players struggling from hole to hole, too stubborn or prideful to ask anyone for advice of any kind. I might have joined them, except that I was so ignorant about the game that I *had* to sign up with a pro just to get the basics down. One day I asked my instructor, Shawn Kelly, if he had ever taken lessons. A few, he answered. But mainly he had "picked the brain" of every player who was better than he. I decided to follow Shawn's lead, watching and questioning (when appropriate) players who had clearly mastered the game. Sure enough, I learned something new every time.

So golf, in a way, is not that different from the process of upgrading managers. The most mature players (think Young Adults) are eager and willing to learn and profit from that attitude. The Adolescents seem content to struggle on their own and pretend to be better than they are.

WHAT TRAINING PROGRAMS MISS

Most organizations today run leadership or educational programs for their managers. In fact, billions of dollars are spent every year by companies worldwide to train and retrain people, to reinvigorate corporate cultures, to redesign organizational structures — to reinvent, recreate and reorganize.

What is remarkable, however, is that most of these efforts fail to make a difference. In a report published in *Consultants News*, only four percent of 242 companies surveyed were very satisfied with the results of such programs. But since no one seems to know what else to do, corporate America keeps spending its money in the same futile way.

The money is being misspent because the training and leadership programs fail to focus on the maturity level of their enrollees. With few exceptions, these programs make no attempt to assess the maturity of managers they are about to instruct. Each enrollee is presumed to be mature, when in fact most are Adolescents of one kind or another.

For management development programs of any kind to succeed, an organization must first determine where each manager fits on the maturity scale and then must tailor its approach accordingly.

In other words, the technique I call "upgrading."

To do otherwise is to spend many thousands of dollars training or educating managers without addressing their ability to use their new found knowledge. This is akin to teaching all students in high school the same classes without regard to their capacity to learn what is being taught. Imagine a freshman being placed in a mathematics class filled with high school seniors.

Absurd! you say.

Of course it is. Yet we do this whenever we assign employees to training courses without any concern for their maturity levels. Our best schools measure the intelligence, attention span, social development and maturity of each student and then attend to each according to his or her needs. Why would a business organization have any less concern for its managers, who represent enormously valuable assets?

10

SUPERCHARGED LEADERSHIP

When I first met Nancy, I was impressed by her sophistication, intelligence and total willingness to be coached. Here indeed was an Adult. She was part of the management team at a technology firm, and her strong leadership skills produced results even with a workforce that at first glance seemed hopeless.

Nancy was often handed the equivalent of the "dirty dozen" — misfits whom no one else could work with. These were the lost souls who had fallen from grace, the staff that no other manager wanted. But under Nancy's leadership, they became different people, willing to do just about anything for her.

How did she accomplish this? My first impressions were these: She treated each person as an individual, not just a cog in the company's machine. She demanded that all pull their weight. She was kind, caring, focused and compassionate. As I worked with Nancy over a period of years, I noted other important aspects of her leadership:

➤ A keen understanding that everyone wants to feel special, coupled with an ability to generate that feeling in the people who worked for her.

➤ A lively sense of humor, which always seemed present.

➤ A determination to find "the best" in others.

➤ A passion to learn something from every encounter or event or challenge.

➤ A commitment to provide her people with constant feedback and coaching, both of which she tailored to actual on-the-job experiences.

➤ Prompt and very public recognition of people when they made important contributions to the team's successes.

Each time I returned to the company, I could see that everyone who had ever worked with Nancy was still fiercely loyal to her. And she continued to reach for new growth experiences, including running a marathon and studying for an MBA. Her belief that her teams could do anything was anchored in that same confidence about herself.

I've told Nancy's story because it illustrates how inseparable leadership is from maturity. No manager can be an effective leader if he or she is mired in immaturity, an Adolescent in mind and spirit. Maturity is the very essence of strong leadership.

Bringing Out "The Best"

Effective leadership is the defining characteristic that separates great corporations from the rest of the pack. Its perfect correlation with the level of management maturity is something I have observed over and over again in my 25 years of working with thousands of executives, supervisors and other managers. In today's business world, it takes a high degree of maturity to make tough decisions, inspire people, deal with complex and changing problems, and maintain balance in one's personal life.

Nobody needs an accomplished leader when the goal is merely to produce acceptable or average results. That's an assignment for the manager who always settles for "getting by." I'm reminded of a client who invariably had ten to twelve weeks of accumulated vacation time, but never took off work for more than a week at a time. When I asked him why, this less-than-effective supervisor replied, "There are only two things that can happen when you're away from your staff and your results, and they're both bad — either things will get worse or they'll get better. I don't want to have either problem to deal with."

But when a company is striving for breakthrough results — the extraordinary, the exceptional, the finest that

145

a workforce has to offer — *real* leadership is an absolute must. I define it as *the ability to bring out "the best" in oneself and in others.* Great leaders do this by:

> *Mobilizing resources.*

> *Identifying and understanding problems and accelerating their solution.*

> *Exciting people to act.*

> *Building morale.*

> *Encouraging people to engage in self-development.*

> *Nurturing the development of others with leadership potential.*

> *Creating a culture of responsibility.*

> *Building a belief in the value of customer service.*

> *Emphasizing the importance of staff loyalty to the organization.*

> *Resolving difficult people problems elegantly.*

I also work from the tested belief that the way to learn how to get "the best" out of people is to get "the best" out of yourself — which brings us right back to maturity. If you can be effective at losing weight, exercising regularly, staying on a healthy diet, quitting cigarettes, finishing your college degree and/or balancing your personal and work lives, you are behaving like a mature Adult. And that is what *real* leaders are all about.

IMMATURITY RUN WILD

Sometimes we lose sight of how critical leadership is to an organization's success. This happened most recently when the value of certain technology stocks, especially those related to the Internet, ballooned out of sight. Millions of investors became incredibly wealthy, at least for a time. But few of them seemed interested in the quality of leadership at these "new economy" companies, and measures of valuation which used to be fundamental to a corporation's relationship to Wall Street were largely ignored. The only question that seemed to warrant discussion was what had the stock done in the last three days?

This lack of attention to corporate leadership had immaturity written all over it. The focus on short-term rewards and the "what's in it for me?" attitude were plainly Adolescent traits. But however unthinking was the behavior of certain investors, they stayed in the game, seemingly oblivious of the approaching bumps in the road. All they cared about was counting their ever-mounting paper profits. It reminded me of teenagers bingeing on beer, or racing hot rods on dark city streets, or engaging in reckless sex.

Savvy business people know that the leadership effectiveness of companies is the ultimate indicator of long-term success or failure. Interestingly, this was demonstrated even as the "gold rush" in techno stocks was gathering steam. A number of "dot.coms" and other technology start-ups began recruiting seasoned executives from mainstream corporate America, essentially to provide some Adult supervision for all the "wunderkids" populating the techno-start-ups.

This usually happened because outside directors, investment bankers or investors themselves demanded it. Sometimes, the company founders themselves recognized the need. Whatever the motivation, it was an acknowledgment that the often-brilliant young founders simply did not have the management skills needed to sustain a company. The creativity and energy that enabled them to develop an idea, find funding and actually launch operations was laudable but not a satisfactory substitute for mature leadership.

TEAM BUILDING
AND MATURITY

Nowhere is mature leadership more important than in the functioning of teams, the social system that has become widely employed by organizations of all kinds. Teams rely on relationships and, like any close knit system of that kind, there is a need for trust, dependability and individual responsibility. The effective leader of a well-functioning team often enables and even requires other members of the team to step forward and assume leadership roles at times. Thus, while there may be a formally designated "team leader," most successful teams function like the proverbial flock of geese, with each member taking his or her turn at leading.

However, while this model is a wonderful concept, it is very difficult to pull off if there are Adolescents on the team, pretending to lead or acting like they think leaders ought to act, or otherwise trying to impress everyone else. A team of individuals working together assumes mature thinking and behavior. In fact, it relies on it!

A team leader needs to be able to recognize any Adolescent tendencies and deal with them up front. If he or she isn't certain if they exist but suspects they might, my advice is to try flushing such behaviors out of hiding. This can be done by watching suspect team members when they are stressed or challenged. If they respond defensively, they may well be Low Functioning Adolescents. A team made up entirely of LFAs is a guaranteed headache for any manager. Expect a maximum number of accidents, miscommunications, excuses and general screw-ups from such a group — just like a band of teenagers assigned to do a job around the house.

Uncovering their comrades, the High Functioning Adolescents, may require more sophisticated detective work, since HFAs can actually *appear* to be leaders. They are terrific at looking good. After all, that's what drives them. They have worked hard to get people to see them as they want to be seen — "cool," together, grown-up and sophisticated. Remember, they view life and work like theatrical parts — wearing the costume for whatever role they are playing. So while someone may appear to be a leader, even a "mature" leader, it is important to confirm that the individual is genuinely competent and wise — not simply the equivalent of a high school student playing the role of Solomon in a pageant.

If the team is mostly comprised of Adolescents, the leader should try to arrange for the participation of at least one Adult who can serve as mentor or coach. The Adult needs to know in advance that he or she will be expected to fill either role and also should be made aware of the team's less mature members. Even if none of the Adults in a team assume a formal role as mentor or coach, they will tend to relate to the Adolescents in that manner anyway. That is the Adult nature — to be supportive, to help others grow. Thus, their presence on a team heightens the probability of maturation gains by Adolescent teammates.

Ultimately, creating and then nurturing a culture in which teams can flourish is *the* job of managers at all levels. The odds of success are best when the person out front is *both* a skilled leader *and* a mature individual.

The Maturity Factor

11

Mastery: Winning the Grand Prize

So now we come to the ultimate reward for those aspiring to Wise Adulthood. I call it "mastery," and I guarantee a rich and fulfilled life at work and at home for any manager who achieves it. Mastery, of course, has to do with an extremely high level of competency. But it is more than that. It is the unrivaled confidence to live life as a wondrous adventure, not a Purgatory on earth that must be endured.

Webster's defines mastery as "dominion" — a word I love because it holds out the promise that we can soar high above the pettiness and anxiety of the Adolescent world. Dominion implies a general transcendence of the need to dominate, a rejection of the notion that we can get what we want by manipulating or coercing others. Dominion is the end game for Adults who are striving to master life.

The search for mastery demands intense observation, patient investigation and diligent research. Young Adults can begin by identifying the patterns that define their lives and then discerning which are healthy and which are not. As they work through this process, the wisest of them will make a fascinating discovery — that life is governed by certain operating principles. Understanding these principles and how to apply them to day-to-day living is a prerequisite to Wise Adulthood.

To Adolescents, all this is a mystery, a matter of magic or pure luck. But in fact, operating principles are universal, like essential laws of Nature. When you follow them, things work and life is smoother and more satisfying. When you don't follow them, things don't go well and life can be frustrating and confusing.

Take, for example, the matter of wealth. When I asked successful business people what they "know" or what they have learned about wealth, many of them told me the same thing. Out of their answers I fashioned this set of operating principles for wealth:

➤ *Money follows value; produce value and money will be attracted to you.*

➤ *"Scarcity thinking," or operating from the perspective that there is never enough money, does not attract money or wealth.*

➤ *Finding something that you're totally passionate about doing is a great way to attract wealth.*

➤ *Loaning money to friends seldom works.*

➤ *Loaning money to family never works.*

➤ *Never underestimate the power of compound interest.*

➤ *Fear never attracts money or wealth.*

➤ *Intelligence and education are not correlated to monetary wealth.*

➤ *Integrity ultimately has greater power to attract money than any other personal characteristic.*

➤ *People with poor integrity often attract some wealth but always pay some unseen penalty.*

You can do the same exercise by selecting an aspect of your life that is especially important to you and then researching the operating principles that apply to it. Not sure what that might be? Here is a list of possibilities:

➤ *Relationships.* ➤ *Physical well-being.*

➤ *Emotional well-being.* ➤ *Sexuality.*

➤ *Travel.* ➤ *Recreation.*

➤ *Spirituality.* ➤ *Exercise.*

➤ *Eating.* ➤ *Drinking patterns.*

➤ *Family.* ➤ *Friends.*

➤ *Lovers/marriage.* ➤ *Parenting.*

> *Falling in love.*   > *Being supervised.*

> *Learning new skills.*   > *Partnering.*

> *Meeting new people.*   > *Supervising others.*

> *Working in a team.*   > *Athleticism.*

> *Working with things.*   > *Competition.*

> *Social graces.*   > *Patience.*

> *Listening.*   > *Consciousness.*

> *Communication.*   > *Language.*

> *Money.*

How you come up with the answers is part of the challenge. But the end results are almost always worth the effort.

MASTERY WITH WEALTH: A VERY SHORT STORY

A successful businessman with whom I consulted for two years never spoke about his wealth

> ## SKILLS OF MASTERY
>
> ➤ Acceptance   ➤ Balance
> ➤ Coachability   ➤ Commitment
> ➤ Discovery Listening   ➤ Enrollment
> ➤ Responsibility   ➤ Intimacy
> ➤ Self-Actualization   ➤ Vision
> ➤ Conscious Intentionality

or his circle of prominent friends and associates. But he always made it a point to ask about *my* life and travels. In one such conversation, we discovered that we were both planning to travel from the New York area to Chicago on the same day. He said it would be enjoyable to make the trip together, and I agreed. It was left up to his secretary take care of reservations.

On the designated day, a limousine picked us up at his office and drove us to a private airport. There we boarded a private jet — his, as it turned out. I was surprised to find I would be flying in such luxury and couldn't suppress a sheepish grin as we boarded. I looked around the cabin and kidded him about my consulting fees being too low. He just smiled.

Nothing more was said about the private jet — what he had paid for it, what it cost to maintain, how much he spent on pilot salaries — on that day or any other. It simply was not something that he thought was worthy of conversation. When I thought about the trip some days later, I realized that this gracious and unassuming man had long ago gotten past the need to convince others of his success. He had clearly reached a level of mastery with money and wealth.

THE SKILLS YOU NEED

Finally, mastery requires certain skills that only Adults, having moving beyond Adolescence, are able to develop. Broadly defined, these skills equip you with the ability to look, listen and observe — not out of a need to simply survive, but out of curiosity and a desire for self-improvement. Each is sharpened with each step you take toward Wise Adulthood. I've touched on some aspects of these skills in earlier chapters. But here is a comprehensive summary that pulls them all together:

BALANCE

Mastery is synonymous with keeping your priorities in balance. The Wise Adult does not allow serious conflict to occur between work and family issues, for example. While others talk about how they would like to spend more time with their families, the Wise Adult finds a way to do it.

Mastery requires inner balance as well. The Wise Adult knows, for example, that everyone possesses qualities that are both masculine and feminine. Note that I'm not saying "male" and "female" here. Rather, I mean a combination that is appropriate to one's gender, incorporating the strength and directness of the masculine with the sensitivity and flexibility of the feminine.

Some women lose balance and sacrifice their femininity when they try to act "powerful" by being forceful. They invariably come across as bullies or men in women's bodies. WA women don't make this mistake. They know that force is not power, it is manipulation. Truly powerful women – like truly powerful men – do not need to be forceful to get what they want and need.

Mastery calls for balance in every aspect of life. To Wise Adults, it's as natural as getting up in the morning.

COACHABILITY

The relatively new profession of "executive coaching" can be a total waste of time if Adolescent managers are the clients. After all, if you are mainly focused on protecting your image, you are going to put all your energies into looking "totally together." But when you act as if you know everything, you can't learn. It's like the Buddhist story of the full-to-the-brim teacup: nothing can be added unless one finds a way to make room for that something more.

Mastery allows one to submit to coaching. In fact, mastery *invites* it! While Adolescents might pretend to be open to coaching, Adults genuinely welcome it, soak it up and grow from it.

COMMITMENT

Adults master the skill of commitment – to make an unconditional promise. They realize that the promise is ultimately made to themselves, and that such a personal promise is far more powerful than one made to another. It takes a mature person, one with a deep sense of responsibility, to make a commitment and keep it.

Adolescents tend to make commitments whenever and wherever it seems to their advantage. Even then, they often confuse *making* a commitment with *keeping* a commitment. Or they let their actions be governed by a sense of *obligation* – the state of having to do something which they have no real motivation or desire to do. But they think they *should*. Sometimes they start out with a purpose in mind but lose sight of it when something more interesting appears on the horizon.

DISCOVERY LISTENING

The ability to really listen has been trained out of most of us. We live in a world that is so frantic that we have become accustomed to communicating by sound-byte – sampling from a dizzying array of inputs. Have you ever been on the phone speaking to someone while checking your e-mails? Or looking at the newspaper?

Enter "Discovery Listening," a term created by my close friend and colleague, Carl Hedleston. His research into listening allowed my firm to design a workshop based on powerful technology that actually teaches people how to listen. Discovery Listening is the ability to temporarily turn off the thoughts that are always flooding your mind — the "internal conversations" mentioned in Chapter Three — so that you can listen to others with your senses at full power. Adults who master this approach are able to absorb not only the words that are being said aloud, but also what is *not* being spoken — but nevertheless is being communicated.

Several years ago I was working with a team of executives and we were in the midst of talking about Discovery Listening. One manager, a woman, said she often didn't feel heard when she talked to her husband. "He only hears what I'm saying," she complained, not realizing how odd that probably sounded to many of the men present. Her point, of course, was that he heard only her spoken words and failed to comprehend the underlying feelings that she was attempting to express.

An oft-repeated truism is that spoken words convey only about seven percent of what others are communicating to us. This leaves 93% for body language, inflection and other ways of getting our feelings across. How many times have you asked someone how they're feeling and you get, "I'm fine" — but every fiber of your being knows that they aren't fine at all? That's Discovery Listening.

The Wise Adult uses Discovery Listening to comprehend what is typically unseen and unheard by the average person. They hear the unspoken and intrinsic. WAs make others feel listened to, understood, like their thoughts matter. People around WAs naturally find themselves wanting to be more open and spontaneous — another reason WAs make such great leaders.

CONSCIOUS INTENTIONALITY

Intentionality is a powerful force. It is where everything starts. Each of our actions or communications are driven by an underlying intention. If the outcome is not what we set out to achieve, it helps to look back at the original intention to see what went wrong. Wise Adults, who are usually quite clear about their intentions, understand the value of this.

In contrast, the intentions of Adolescents can be clouded since what drives them is the desire to impress others and avoid embarrassment. It is no wonder that their outcomes are often at considerable odds with what they thought they wanted – adding further to their confusion.

Following a conscious intention to a successful conclusion requires that you have a vision in mind, a mental picture of what you are pursuing. Virtually all of our greatest contemporary athletes use some form of visualization in training and competition. They have a clear goal in mind, and the intense desire to accomplish that goal is assurance that their intentions will not waver. Adults have mastery over this. They create visions for themselves and then work diligently to make them happen.

Remember President Kennedy's speech challenging the nation to put a man on the moon within a decade? It was a classic example of conscious intentionality with a desired outcome; no one knew how it would happen, but the President's determination to see it through became the collective will, and success followed.

INTIMACY

It's a subject that may seem out of place in a book about business and organizational life, but intimacy is a key skill for achieving mastery. One cannot be open to growth, to learning and to being coached, unless one can be intimate. Now, I don't mean physical intimacy or sex. Webster's defines intimate as "characterizing one's deepest nature." So you could say being intimate is being authentic, the genuine article, someone who can be trusted implicitly.

Aren't these the traits you would like to see in close friends, co-workers and most everyone else with whom you associate? Well, if you are an Adult, you'd probably answer "yes." But Adolescents can be and often are intimidated by intimacy. After all, people could then see their insecurity and fear of being found out. Intimacy is the last thing they want, and that, sad to say, prevents them from mastering life.

SELF-ACTUALIZATION

Wise Adults know their inadequacies or insecurities but don't live in terror of them like Adolescents. In their state of self-actualization, WAs face their demons with courage and determination whenever they appear.

Self-actualized Wise Adults don't waste time covering up. They know that by doing so they are only hurting themselves and slowing their spiritual, emotional and intellectual growth. Since their growth in these areas is high among their priorities, they will not do anything to hinder it, unlike Adolescents. This consciousness prevails in the Wise Adult.

VISION

Vision is quite different from merely having a goal. Vision comes with much less emotional attachment but demands huge commitment. Sound paradoxical? It is. But bear with me. A goal triggers expectations that can become quite vivid in the imagination of the goal-setter. If the expectations are sufficiently intense, the goal-setter will have a huge emotional investment in the outcome. All energies will be focused on turning the goal into reality; any alternative course of action that might be more sensible or desirable will have no chance of consideration.

But mastery requires an ability to pursue something without getting so fixated on a certain result that all other possibilities are crowded out. This is the skill called vision, and it allows miracles to occur that one may never have imagined. It means we can remain open to new ideas, ready to let forces from any direction come into play, even as we follow a well-thought-out course of action.

Wise Adults are often pleasantly surprised by how their visions change shape and finally play out and share in the wonder of the creative process. They find it fun and exciting, and they aim high with their visions, sometimes daring to pursue quite audacious outcomes.

Surprise is a threat for Adolescents, though, and they never find the vision process to their liking. They tend to aim low to avoid failure or the appearance of failure, and you will often hear them say at strategic planning meetings, "We've got to be realistic." Adolescents tend to see a particular goal as the only one that is "right," whereas Wise Adults see it as a good possibility – but perhaps only one of several that might come along.

ENROLLMENT

When Wise Adults want to attract others to their point of view, they purposely avoid hard-sells or otherwise imposing their opinions on others. Instead, they "enroll" support by offering their views or describing their visions and then listening to the objections – really listening, in a Discovery Listening way. They do not try to make their case in a classic debative or argumentative manner. They remain flexible, open to change and ready to consider everyone's input. While they know what they would prefer, they are far less attached to any specific outcome than the Adolescents, who will do their best to "sell" their ideas.

ACCEPTANCE

WAs have learned how to be accepting of unexpected developments or events. When the playing field tilts in one direction or another, they react calmly and reapply their creative energies. This is not a weakness or a lack of commitment; their vision remains quite clear. Rather, it is a sign of their ability to be flexible when determining the specific form that a solution may take. The WAs remain focused on results and are not thrown off balance when the process to obtain those results becomes a bit more challenging.

A good example, once again, is President Kennedy's declaration that Americans would explore the moon. The visionaries behind the project, the leaders of NASA, scoured the scientific community for thoughts on how to do it — what the space vehicle would look like, what fuel it would use, and so on. They knew they had to be flexible in planning each step, lest they overlook a first-rate idea. But they never let the process divert their focus from their vision, a successful moon landing.

RESPONSE-ABLE

I once heard the word "responsible" defined as having to do with one's ability to respond. It amused me and I thought, why not? I played with the idea and came up with my own invention: "response-able," meaning the ability to refrain from reacting automatically, or compulsively, or obsessively. Think of being able to put yourself into a mental state in which you invariably respond with clear-mindedness and a total lack of preconception to whatever comes into your life.

Wise Adults know how to do this. They no longer have any axes to grind, and they have less "baggage" to protect or defend. Wise Adults respond.

But not Adolescents. Most have pre-programmed themselves to react automatically to situations, especially when their images or their feelings might be exposed. They can't be spontaneous or neutral in the way they respond. They *react* rather than *respond*.

Adolescents constantly feel victimized by situations that Adults turn to their advantage. Adults listen and observe life while Adolescents just react to what is going on around them. Imagine that you're a dog, and every time you see your owner you get fed or petted. Soon, your response is totally predictable. You automatically react when stimulated. That's the life that most Adolescents are destined to live — over and over.

It's All Connected

By now, you've probably seen that several relationships exist between these skills.

For instance, Vision is closely linked to Intentionality. Discovery Listening is a pathway to Intimacy, which in turn is impacted by Vision. A lack of Vision leaves little possibility for Intimacy to flourish and may even kill it.

Acceptance is a major part of Enrollment and Commitment. They all go hand in glove and one can't work without the others.

How effective are you in practicing each of these skills? Might you be doing well in some and not in others? Becoming adept at just one or another of them is not mastery, especially if the motivation is to build a protective image.

Wise Adults seek true mastery. They know they must learn to keep all these skills in delicate balance.

PEOPLE I ADMIRE

We all have role models, and here are a few of mine — people I admire tremendously for their "Wise Adult-ness":

WARREN BUFFET

He embodies all that is classically American: he is wealthy beyond most people's imaginations and has succeeded in virtually everything he has done over the last forty years. He is a generous man who contributes large amounts of money to causes and ideas he believes in. He does not court public attention; Buffet is seldom seen on television and, unlike some of his contemporaries, does not have businesses, buildings or airlines named after him.

THE DALAI LAMA

The spiritual leader of Tibet, he was exiled many years ago by the Chinese government. From every country and venue possible, he continues to preach tolerance, openness and the hope that his homeland will be freed from Chinese rule. He lives a life uncluttered by possessions. Status matters not. He is kind, caring and willing to share his ideas with anyone who is interested. And, he is clearly a happy man.

COLIN POWELL

Retired Chairman of the Joint Chiefs and now Secretary of State, General Colin Powell is an outstanding example of a Wise Adult. Despite being courted as a presidential or vice presidential prospect by leading politicians, he was resolute in focusing his energies elsewhere — especially doing good for children with the America's Promise Foundation. When he agreed to serve in the Bush Cabinet, he opted for statesmanship over politics. While I don't know the General personally, I presume that he saw politics as the Adolescent game that it is and chose instead to serve his country in other ways.

JOHN CHAMBERS

CEO of Cisco Systems since 1995, John Chambers has created additional shareholder value of over $480 billion. He was featured in the May 15,

2000, issue of *Fortune* magazine, which placed him at the top level of "greatest CEOs." The magazine credited him with making Cisco one of the world's outstanding companies.

MOTHER TERESA

For obvious reasons, Mother Teresa makes this list. She completely dedicated herself and her life to working with the poor and with children. She raised money and attracted support for her causes from thousands of people, without ever displaying a selfish motive. Her willingness to make personal sacrifices so that she could be of service to others was truly inspiring.

STEVEN SPIELBERG

He impresses me because of his personal and professional successes, and his commitment to sharing his wealth in the service of causes that he supports. He is, by all accounts, a humble person who eschews the public spotlight in favor of remaining in the background.

Oprah Winfrey

Despite being one of the wealthiest and most powerful figures in the U.S. media, she made a very public commitment to her own development as a human being. On her TV talk show, she transcended her Jerry Springer-like persona to become someone genuinely committed to helping people recover from past woundings and grow spiritually. She was not afraid to let her vulnerability show, sharing her remarkable transformation with millions of viewers each day.

You may have noticed that some of the richest people in the world did not make the list. This is intentional. Just because someone has amassed a great fortune does not make them an Adult. In fact, being really rich may be counter-correlated to maturity. Many Adolescents accumulate wealth as a means of proving themselves, of looking *really* good, like they can't get enough validation. They use their wealth as a scorecard to prove they are okay. Donald Trump is a great example of a High Functioning Adolescent who puts great stock in his wealth, his wives or girlfriends and other external trappings.

12

Putting Adult Thinking into Action

W ondering how to apply Adult thinking to your everyday life? Here are some tips from an interview, explaining how Adult thinking can help you become more successful in business and even enhance your personal relationships.

Question– This is a big subject. Where do we start, Larry?

Answer– With the basics. If I've learned anything in life, it is this: when I confront my pain or upset directly, it usually passes quickly and growth begins. So a good starting point is to take the measure of yourself, your maturity, and your opportunities to grow.

Q– But when do we get to the tips?

A– Be patient. The idea is to first make you think differently and more deeply. You need to ask the most penetrating and insightful questions of yourself. Think of it as preparation for what will follow.

Q– Hmm ... I think I get it. But what kind of questions?

A– Here are two tough ones: What areas of your life are you blind in, or avoiding, because of real or potential emotional or psychological pain? Where are your weaknesses most obvious in your life?

Q– How about some that might help me better understand my strengths?

A– I have two favorites: What insights and growth have you had in the past that you might now be overlooking and that you might draw on again? Where are your strengths least used or least applied in your life?

Q– Any more?

A– Indeed, but I want them to come from you. Take some time later to think up some of your own. Go for truly penetrating questions that will give you new perspectives or information about yourself. It's a great exercise in self-understanding. And by the way, others can help. Think of who knows the most about you, your behavior and maturity, and then ask this question: Are you making the most effective use of that person's insights?

Q– This is all very intriguing. But I thought we were talking about applying Adult thinking to my everyday life?

A– We are! All these questions that I've posed are part of a process to get us there. Think of it as creating operating principles for every aspect of your life – including your job and your personal relationships. The operating principles make possible the application of Adult thinking, day in and day out.

Q– How about a real-life example?

A– Let's talk about sales professionals. In the last 25 years, I've worked with and trained literally thousands of them. It's a field that attracts many who are psychologically and emotionally immature – virtual Adolescents. They are all wrapped up in themselves, they think all they need to succeed is energy, and their main goal is to make a ton of money quickly. Most end up demoralized or rejected within a few short months. The true professionals, on the other hand, see sales as something more – a challenging occupation that demands maturity, personal growth and dedication. They understand that their success is measured by long-term results rather than the returns for one month. This is Adult thinking at its best.

Q– And they get to that point by pursuing this process of self-examination or continual learning that you talked about earlier?

A– Right. They make mistakes, but learn from them. In the process, they discover something about the nature of selling that eludes the Adolescents – that selling is an expression of partnership and relationship with the client. It has nothing to do with trying to get people to buy your product or service, per se.

Q– What happens when they make that discovery?

A– Well, it is an insight that changes the nature of client relationships forever. The sales professional begins to find ways to nurture these relationships without worrying about immediate results. The big difference between Adolescents and Adults who sell for a living is that Adults realize their job is to understand and appreciate each real or potential client. And then it is their purpose to know each as a person, and to make each feel special when they are together.

Q– But what about rejection, something everyone in sales experiences?

A— For the Adolescent, rejection creates confusion, fear and doubt. But the Adult sales professional comes away with a greater sense of purpose and an enhanced understanding of how to cope with what has happened. Every great sales person can tell you stories about disheartening rejections that ultimately led to a long and prosperous relationship with clients.

Q— So if you had to list some operating principles for sales professionals that reflected Adult thinking, what would they be?

A— I can think of several. In no particular order, they are:

> ➤ *It's all about relationships.*

> ➤ *Great products and services only sell themselves for a while.*

> ➤ *A client who feels special to you will make you feel special sooner or later.*

> ➤ *When a client has no money and no time to see you, spend time with the client's secretaries and support staff. Make these people feel special.*

> ➤ *When a client has money and time to see you, spend time with the client's secretaries and support staff. Make these people feel special.*

> ➤ *If you create a problem for a client, tell him or her quickly,*

> take responsibility for it, and find out what must be done to keep the client feeling special.

> ➤ If you lie to a client, a client will lie to you.

> ➤ Create partnerships and relationships for life and your life will get easier over time.

Q– That sure covers a lot of ground. Any other examples of how to apply Adult thinking in business?

A– Let me start with an example of non-Adult thinking. We have all seen managers who make the people under them miserable. They are insecure souls who are always worried about not getting the next promotion or not making enough money. They behave like slave drivers, using emotional terrorism to get their way. They are ill-equipped – both emotionally and psychologically – to be supervising anyone.

Q– And the flip side?

A– The flip side, of course, is managers who apply Adult thinking in almost everything they do. Again, their mistakes turn into learning and their learning turns into success. They have the ability to bring out the best in themselves and others.

Q– Give me some specifics.

A– Feedback is one. It works both ways with them. They give corrective feedback quickly and objectively. They seek constructive feedback constantly. Also, when confronting a problem of their own making, they do it without becoming defensive. And they do it with a clear sense of their purpose, which is to do better and not repeat their error.

Q– Any other thoughts on these Adult-thinking managers?

A– Here's a very important point: they understand the importance of their personal well-being, of maintaining some basic life balance. This means that work is not always their top priority 24 hours a day. It means taking time to exercise, to meditate, to relax, to be with family and friends.

Q– Sounds reasonable, but isn't it hard to do sometimes?

A– Yes, it can be, especially if it's not really supported in the workplace. I can't tell you how many corporate vision statements I've read that say something about "having our employees be well" or "run our business so that our staff can live whole and complete lives."

But the sad truth is that very few organizations do much of anything to promote these values. So you have to be responsible for this yourself.

Q– And if you lose your sense of "life balance," as you put it?

A– It can make you miserable. For example, if you're too busy to work out or you're traveling and don't manage your food intake well, you can quickly gain weight. If you're highly stressed and have no way to release the stress, you may find yourself suppressing emotions and feelings, and even overeating.

Q– Back to the managers who apply Adult thinking. Can you list some operating principles for them?

A– Well, many are contained in my earlier answers, like understanding that mistakes and failures are really opportunities for learning and growth. But here are a few of my other favorites:

➤ *Demonstrate your beliefs through your actions, and assess everyone who works for you according to that standard.*

➤ *The capacity to be inspired is the most inspirational quality of all.*

➢ *Not everyone is going to be an "A" player, or a great employee. Adjust your actions accordingly.*

➢ *Over-communicate whenever possible.*

➢ *Listen more than you talk.*

➢ *Bring out the best in others by pressing them for their best and treating them fairly.*

➢ *Always have a mentor or coach or both.*

➢ *What gets measured will always get done first.*

Q– Let's switch gears here and talk about applying Adult values to personal relationships. How does that work?

A– The process is really no different from what we've been discussing. You must establish operating principles for your relationships and then act on them.

Q– So we need some questions first, like the ones we started with?

A– Right. You might, for example, start with this: How would I assess my overall maturity in my personal relationships? Then flip the question and ask yourself, how would those whom I love, trust and respect rate me in those same relationships?

Q– These can be difficult questions to answer, I think.

A– Some of the most challenging have to do with identifying Adolescent behavior in yourself. Here are two examples: What Adolescent patterns do I exhibit in my personal relationships? What are the conditions or circumstances which bring out those patterns?

Q– After you go through this self-assessment process, what's next?

A– You have to determine what you can do to improve your most important relationships – how to transform yourself, in so many words. I'm a big believer in coaching and mentoring at this stage. Outsiders bring a whole new energy and perspective to the process. So you might start thinking about who your coach or mentor could be.

Q– Let's assume that I now have a good understanding of Adult thinking in relationships. Do you have some examples of how I might apply it?

A– Sure. Let's talk about raising children. I have several operating principles that I've learned from interviewing successful parents. I'll just list them:

➤ *Every child is different and needs to be treated differently.*

➤ Children get their "programming" from everything and everybody they have contact with when they're young – it matters what they hear from their friends and see on TV and at the movies.

➤ Discipline is the application of predefined consequences that are applied immediately and dispassionately when a child violates a rule.

➤ Parental emotion can sometimes undermine discipline. The problem is that children often hear the message of anger (I don't love you now) rather than the message about their behavior.

➤ Create a stable and thoughtful environment for children until they reach puberty, and the chances are good that they will get through it with little difficulty.

➤ Listening to a child with all of your attention teaches them how to listen.

➤ When children win, they need and deserve encouragement and love. When they lose or fail, they need and deserve encouragement and love.

➤ If you create a successful friendship with a child at an early age, you will be showing that child how to do the same with others as he or she grows older.

Q– Some of these require a real effort by parents, don't they? But I suppose that is what Adult thinking is all about.

A– You're right. Take, for example, the really critical issue of children having access to all kinds of experiences. Too many parents tend to push their children toward activities that the parents have a passion for, whether it be a favorite sport or a career choice. It's an understandable urge, I guess. But parents who do that deprive their children of a full range of experiences, including whatever the parents haven't known or don't like. Let the children show us what their interests and their aptitudes are. And then we, as adults, can celebrate their success, even though it might not be the "success" that we have in mind for them. That's an excellent application of Adult thinking.

Q– How about relationships between spouses. Any thoughts?

A– In my leadership workshops, I often ask people about their spouses or loved ones. I want to know what are their secrets to success. The ones who demonstrate Adult thinking are focused on finding ways to keep things fresh and alive with their partners.

Q– What are their "secrets of success?"

A– All sorts of things. For example:

➤ *Have a "date" with your spouse one weekend night each month. Spouses alternate planning the date. Both must make it a top priority.*

➤ *Look for a new hobby or avocation that the two of you can do together.*

➤ *Have a quarterly "retreat weekend" that is totally focused on recreating connection and intimacy between partners.*

➤ *Spend some time each night just letting one person talk while the other listens.*

➤ *Write poetry or prose to each other.*

➤ *On your wedding anniversary or other special date, write vows that express your feelings of love, caring and connection.*

➤ *Hold hands.*

➤ *Take baths together, with candles, flowers and special scents all around you.*

Q– It's a fascinating list.

A– It can certainly help you get some perspective on yourself and even measure your level of maturity. I expect some people would read the list and say, "These are great! Some couples really are inventive." But others would say, "Oh, my God. This is too much!" Depending on how you react, you might or might not be ready to

take your intimate relationships to the next levels of
personal connection.

Q– Again, help me make the connection between this and
Adult thinking.

A– When you apply Adult thinking to personal relationships,
you are constantly focusing on making your partner
feel as special as he or she really is. You find the time
to say "Thanks" or "I love you" or "I appreciate you"
– all the things that express connection and intimacy.
Real Adults never let that bond fall by the wayside.
They find ways to keep coupled and joined emotionally
even when they're not together.

Q– Thanks for a great interview, Larry. Any last thoughts
before we close?

A– The most important ingredient in Adult thinking is
having the commitment and courage to look at yourself
carefully and completely, to examine your own personal
maturity. Add to that the ability to transform any event,
even the worst setback, into a significant learning experience.
The rest will fall into place if you work at it every day.

13

Conclusion, but Not "The End"

In parting, I offer two laws that you can take to the bank, as the saying goes. Let's call them "Liberty's Laws" for the sake of my own gratification. Liberty's Laws are:

Any business that conducts an effective self-assessment of its leadership maturity gains an immediate strategic advantage in the marketplace.

AND

Be very cautious about entering into business relationships with Adolescents – the cost could be worse than your wildest imagination.

Now I don't mean to minimize the effort required to follow my advice, especially the first law. Measuring and then upgrading the maturity of executives, key managers and other leaders is a big undertaking. A business must have the courage to uncover and then face up to its own strengths and weaknesses. And it must be willing to make a hard, dispassionate estimate of its true chances for success and failure. The challenge will always be how fully, completely and accurately the organization is able to accomplish all this.

But armed with the results, a business has the opportunity to see inside of itself for perhaps the first time. It can accurately discern what behaviors will make it a more successful competitor. It can begin to rid itself of those managers who will not or cannot grow into maturity.

Imagine the company in which managers are not distracted by personal insecurities and chronic defensiveness, where the Adults in charge display creativity and professionalism and value interdependence and collegiality. Imagine the company in which petty gossip, back-stabbings and the constant refrain of excuses are not present. Imagine the company that puts a premium on the emotional and intellectual maturity of its workforce. Isn't that what we all want and deserve?

The rules that govern businesses have undergone startling changes in the last decade. Old indicators of success have lost their importance. How long a company has existed — its history, its tradition — used to be a point of pride. Now companies that are only weeks old become darlings of Wall Street (though sometimes fading nearly as fast). Profitability used to be an important indicator of success.

It still is in many quarters, but the experience of some Internet companies has shown that some treat it as a quaint but outmoded concept.

When the ground is shifting this fast, no organization can tolerate Adolescent management. A company that fails to put a premium on leadership maturity will be left in the evolutionary dust while its more farsighted competitors take over.

But the challenge does not end with organizations. There is a broader human dimension as well — a deep yearning in all of us to find meaning in our lives. This yearning is what makes us human - it is what drives our quest for expansion, growth and knowledge.

But it cannot be satisfied if we continue to tolerate immaturity in the way we relate to each other, the way we work together, the way we identify ourselves as individuals, communities and even countries. We cannot continue to choose short-term gratification over long-term sustainability. We cannot progress as a people unless there are Adults to repair the damage done by Adolescents.

Use this book to become an advocate of psychological and emotional maturation — the key to improving your own well-being and the well-being of your family, your friends, your work team and your company. Become a more mature person and you will become one of those people who makes the world a better place. You're not required to have all the answers to mankind's problems, or to rise to a position of great power, like a president of a country. All you need to do is take a stand – make a commitment to be all you can as a person first and a leader second. It all starts with you and the choices you make right now.

BIBLIOGRAPHY &
RECOMMENDED READING

The following books have been instrumental in shaping my thinking as I developed the ideas in *The Maturity Factor*. In some cases they helped clarify notions and concepts through similar or complimentary ideas, i.e. Goleman's work. In some cases they simply gave me a broader context from which I was able to grow or refine my own experience, i.e. Peter Block's *The Empowered Manager*. In others my own personal path and growth were accelerated, giving me access to new insights and intuition that helped me understand the world.

I am often asked what books I recommend people should read. My response is to go to the web or the bookstore and spend a couple of hours looking, feeling, sensing, and reviewing as many books as possible. Pick the top two or three and then read them from cover to cover. I have found that doing this once a month or once a quarter will greatly expand one's awareness and sharpen one's thinking. To all of the authors listed below I say thank you for your work and for making your experience and thinking public. Creating meaningful ideas and concepts is one thing. Putting them into readable forms is quite another.

Scott Adams, *The Dilbert Principle* (New York: HarperBusiness) 1996

Karl Albrecht, *The Only Thing That Matters* (New York: HarperBusiness) 1992

Angles Arrien, *The Four-fold Way, Walking the Paths of the Warrior, Teacher, Healer, and Visionary* (San Francisco: HarperSanFrancisco) 1993

Warren Bennis, *Why Leaders Can't Lead* (San Francisco: Jossey-Bass) 1989

Peter Block, *The Empowered Manager* (San Francisco: Jossey-Bass) 1987

Laurence Boldt, *Zen and the Art of Making a Living* (New York: Penguin) 1991

Fritjof Capra, *The Turning Point, Science, Society, and the Rising Culture* (Toronto: Bantam Books) 1982

James Champy, *Reengineering Management* (New York: HarperCollins) 1995

Deepak Chopra, *Creating Health* (Boston: Houghton Mifflin Company) 1987

Stephen Covey, *The 7 Habits of Highly Effective People* (New York: Simon and Schuster) 1989

Stan Davis, Bill Davidson, *2002 Vision, Transform Your Business Today to Succeed in Tomorrow's Economy* (New York: Simon & Schuster) 1991

David H. Freedman, *The 30 Management Principles of the U.S. Marines* (New York: HarperBusiness) 2000

Murray Gell-Mann, *The Quark and the Jaguar* (New York: W.H.Freeman and Company) 1994

Daniel Goleman, *Working with Emotional Intelligence* (New York: Bantam Books) 1998

Erich Harth, *The Creative Loop, How the Brain Makes a Mind* (Reading: Addison-Wesley) 1993

James E. Liebig, *Merchants of Vision, People Bringing New Purpose and Values to Business* (San Francisco: Berrett-Koehler Publishers) 1994

Dudley Lynch, & Paul Kordis, *Strategy of the Dolphin* (New York: William Morrow & Company) 1988

David McNally, *Even Eagles Need a Push* (New York: Delacorte Press) 1990

Michael Hammer, *The Agenda* (New York: Random House) 2001

Michael Le Boeuf, *Imagineering, How to Profit from your Creative Powers* (New York: McGraw-Hill Book Company) 1982

Michael Lewis, *NEXT* (New York: W.W. Norton & company) 2001

John Maxwell, *The 17 Indisputable Laws of Teamwork* (Nashville: Thomas Nelson Publishers) 2001

Miyamoto Musashi, *A Book of Five Rings* (New York: The Overlook Press) 1982

Mara Selvini Palazzoli, *The Hidden Games of Organizations* (New York: Pantheon Books) 1986

Scott Peck, *The Road Less Traveled* (New York: Touchstone) 1978

Tom Peters, *Thriving on Chaos* (New York: Alfred A. Knopf) 1987

Steven Pinker, *How the Mind Works* (New York: W.W. Norton & Company) 1997

Michael Ray, Alan Rinzler, *The New Paradigm in Business* (New York: G.P. Putnam's Sons) 1993

Wess Roberts, *Leadership Secrets of Attila the Hun* (New York: Warner Books) 1985

Don Miguel Ruiz, *The Mastery of Love, A Practical Guide to the Art of Relationship* (San Rafael, Amber-Allen Publishing) 1999

Ron Schultz, *Unconventional Wisdom* (New York: HarperBusiness) 1974

Peter Senge, *The Fifth Discipline* (New York: Doubleday) 1990

John Stevens, *Abundant Peace, the Biography of Morihei Ueshiba* (Boston: Shambhala) 1987

Eckhart Tolle, *Practicing The Power of Now* (Novato: New World Library) 1999

Michael Treacy, Fred Wiersema, *The Discipline of Market Leaders* (Reading: Addison-Wesley) 1995

Chogyam Trungpa, *Shambhala: The Sacred Path of the Warrior* (Boston: Shambhala Publications) 1984

David Viscott, *Emotionally Free* (Chicago: Contemporary Books) 1992

Harry Woodward, Steve Buckholz, *After-Shock, Helping People through Corporate Change* (New York: John Wiley & Sons) 1987

ABOUT THE AUTHOR

L arry Liberty, Ph.D., has over twenty-five years experience as a consultant in the areas of individual and organizational effectiveness. He is the founder of The Liberty Consulting Team and has personally trained and consulted with over 100,000 managers and staff members, serving as a personal coach to numerous executives. His articles have been widely published and he is a sought-after speaker, educator and lecturer because of his ability to weave powerful principles and ideas together with tested practices. He is personally committed to making learning and growth be engaging, challenging and fun. Liberty is also the author of *Leadership Wisdom: A Guide to Producing Extraordinary Results*.

After graduating from college, he served in the Peace Corps in Brazil. He then worked for the State of California while pursuing his Masters Degree in Public Administration. Liberty then joined Kepner-Tregoe consultants for seven years. He earned his M.A. in 1976 and served as an executive for Landmark Education.

In 1981, he created The Liberty Consulting Team and began working toward his doctoral degree. He became a principle consultant to NASA in the study and development of a new technology for creating High Performance Teams who would man the orbiting space stations of the future. In 1984, he earned his Ph.D. in Organizational Behavior. Throughout his career, Liberty's clients have included:

ATT	American Express
Bank of America	Boeing
Brookings Institute	California Highway Patrol
CBS	Chrysler
Citibank	Department of Air Force
Department of Navy	Fed Executive Board
First Chicago Bank	Internal Revenue Service (IRS)
Kodak	Kaiser Permanente
Levi Strauss	Lucent
Pacific Bell	Proctor & Gamble
NASA	SmithKline Laboratories
Solomon Brothers	Sprint
Stanford University Hospital	United Airlines
US Congress	Warner-Lambert

APPENDIX C

CONTACT INFORMATION

The Liberty Consulting Team

2120 Shelfield Dr.

Carmichael, CA 95608

(916)484-6463

www.libertyconsulting.com

31876490R00126

Made in the USA
Middletown, DE
15 May 2016